The Daculi Witch Chronicles

Kat Ricker

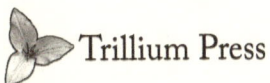 Trillium Press

Thank you to Alana Kujala, for believing in this book.

Editor   John C. Ricker
Cover Design & Production   Tom Sumner

Published on 31 October, 2010.

©2010 Trillium Press
Portland, Oregon
www.MightyKat.net
ISBN 978-0-615-34669-4

Watch the trailer for this book at www.MightyKat.net/DWC

Dedicated to Alana, Christy, my mother,
and strong women everywhere.

Some stories are true that never happened.

—Elie Weisel

-1-

The Secret of Queen Elizabeth

Her new tutor had arrived. Elizabeth slipped into the chamber behind him and watched him set up books on the heavy oak table. He unpacked two inkpots and quill pens and set them carefully within reach. She noticed that he did not smooth the feathers like most men. She greeted him in Latin. He turned and bowed formally.

"My Lady Elizabeth," he answered in Latin. "As you surely know, I am your tutor, William Grindal. How is it that you have learned Latin?"

"Fine beginning question. But moreover, how is it that you have learned yours?" He raised his dark brows.

"I am a graduate of Cambridge."

"Latin is a necessary language for the educated man to possess, " she said. "Perhaps you are of the persuasion that it is more lovely than English, and also truer to itself."

He unfolded his curule. Somewhat outdated but still handsome, this iron chair had literally supported him through decades of study. The traces of a smile played on his face. Her eyes lit briefly on the curule. She did not react to his breech of conduct, sitting before she did, but instead took her own seat, gracefully gathering her skirt below her. The chair raised her to the table beside him; her satin slippers pointed toward the floor.

Speaking now in English, he opened the books before them.

"I am of the persuasion that regardless of how clever talk may be, it is in no way a substitute for true intellectual pursuit. Now, we will begin with the sciences."

Thus began their ritual morning study. For years they would keep this routine. Elizabeth rose a few hours beforehand for prayer with her brother Edward. Though solemn, it was a time of private delight the two shared, gazing into each other's eyes, checking the wellness in each other's pallor, kneeling quietly without interruption and holding hands for hours at a time. Often they would then study together, sitting beside one another and reading from thick volumes in the blue light of the rising sun. Then they would eat breakfast and go each to their tutor, fortified and ready to thrust themselves into their learning with impressive intensity. Study was followed by the midday meal and then young Edward went outside for exercise and Elizabeth to her private chamber to play the lute, or the viol, as took her interest, and sometimes needlepoint. Often she found herself reopening the books that they had just closed, and recreating the lessons from Grindal still active in her mind.

Grindal was well-respected in the household, and thought to be the very cream of scholars to instruct eleven year-old Elizabeth. It soon became apparent that his knowledge superceded even his education, an inexplicable but undeniable fact, thus making him unfathomably erudite besides formally lettered. His manners were impeccable. *A true gentleman*, the women often remarked. Besides this, his distinguished swarthy looks were noted, openly by Blanche Parry, who was old enough to say such things without consequence. But even Katherine Champernowne, Elizabeth's governess, who was quite established with John Ashley, was seen to eye him in a questionable way. Elizabeth took to calling him Grindal, and soon it became the adopted practice, although his subordinates and sticklers of etiquette, such as the governess Katherine, were exceptions. To her, he was "Sir Grindal" and would remain so for all the years of his stay.

Katherine, also nicknamed Kat by Elizabeth, conducted Elizabeth as if she were her own. It was she who first taught Elizabeth her letters, how to both read and to write them. It was she who saw to it that the young princess was properly attired. It was she who made sure Elizabeth was in bed at a suitable hour. And it was she who saw to it that her lady was respected as a queen, although it had been only last year, 1544, that she and her sister Mary had been restored to their seats in line for the throne, by the King's Henrician Act of Succession. Had this change made any marked effect on Elizabeth's character?

"My lady has always commanded respect." Kat told Grindal one day. "Were the most notorious rogue to pass her on the street, he would feel compelled to remove his hat and wait while she passed, even without knowing her status."

Grindal taught Elizabeth French, Italian, some Greek, and furthered her Latin until at thirteen years old, Elizabeth was a deft translator both from Latin to English and the other way round. They studied the liberal sciences, moral teachings, classical studies, and timely Humanism. Morality was riddled with the pitting of Protestantism against Catholicism, and Elizabeth found her comfort there.

"It is not so much that one claim a religion, as one must claim conviction," she proclaimed.

Grindal had been recounting to Elizabeth the particulars of the Reformation, and her eyes had trailed off sometime ago. She interrupted Grindal.

"Must one claim this for one's own clarity or for one's appearance in the eyes of others?" she asked.

He paused and looked up from his book.

"Both amount to one's own satisfaction." He drew himself up, the thickness of his doublet not masking the strong lines of his carriage. "Such a line of thinking may appear a simple and direct route to an end result, your satisfaction. In fact, the two natures of the end are across an immeasurable abyss. If you find yourself standing completely on one side of this abyss, the crossing will be impossible."

"You question my want of satisfaction."

"I encourage you to examine the nature of this satisfaction. Then, if a direct route is what you seek, the technique is to approach the ends with the appropriate means. To mismatch these is to erect immediate impediments. Examine before moving. Now to examine your learning of the Reformation."

She recounted in perfect detail everything he had told her. Her performance as a rule demonstrated a mixture of diligence and acuity, and therefore when she was in the least bit off par, it was obvious.

One such day found Grindal's pupil slow in answers, a slowness coupled with unmaskable distraction that compelled him to finally close his book.

"Elizabeth, something other than grammar commands your mind. If you cannot concentrate, neither of us profits. Perhaps you would like to tell me what it is."

She looked to him, startled. The slant of light through the glass window fell over her well-molded cheekbone, her chin resting against her shapely pink arm. She blinked.

"If you would like to tell me what you are thinking of, perhaps we can think it through together more quickly."

She looked down at the closed book and then at the wood

of the table.

"I am sorry. I do not mean to throw away our time." Her eyes fixed on him resolutely bright, albeit unconvincingly so. His black eyes held her steadily, their dark lashes keeping the light. Her gaze wavered, and she threw it toward the window. Then she felt the heavy warmth of his hand on her forearm.

"If you would like to tell me, I would like to know," he said.

His hand was strongly chiseled, a carpenter's hand, pleasantly incongruous with the rich intellectual handsomeness of his face. Her heart beat a little faster. The dinner bell rang, and with it came the sure steps of Kat to fetch her mistress. The decision of an instant lit in Elizabeth's face.

"Come to my chamber after dinner. I will talk to you, if you wish to know."

≈

Her private chamber was more ornate than their study chamber, with rich woven tapestries and gleaming baroque chairs.

Grindal stepped inside with no apparent notice of his surroundings and walked straight to the settee, seating himself with familiarity, singularly intent on his mission. She has glad to see the mood had sustained through the meal, and he was still willing to hear what she had to say. She stood over the lamp, fingering it idly, her long, slender fingers touched by its glow. She obviously did not know how to begin.

"I won't talk until you're finished, " he assured her. "You may say what you like."

She smiled. She wasn't accustomed to being lost for words.

"Why don't you sit down? You may as well be as comfortable as I am."

He did have a way of charming her. She smiled at him this time and sat beside him. He waited.

"It has come under my attention," she said, "that there seem to be certain matters that are in this house unmentioned, that somehow I feel it would be unwelcome of me to broach, and yet, these matters, they are matters that I may well have questions about . . ." She paused and smoothed her skirt. "I do, in fact, have questions, and can only wonder whether the results are politically heinous, or insulting to some member of our house, or if perhaps the truth is something so hideous, so repulsive, that . . . These matters, you see, are not matters that can forever be kept from my grasp. Once my time has come and I move among the outside world, not just in these sheltered precincts, these are the very matters, which, if questionable, will certainly be addressed and redressed to me. That is why, aside from any private curiosities I may harbor, I should possess the whole bald truth."

Her cheeks flushed with awareness that someone had finally heard thoughts which had long been only hers. Grindal remained looking at her with the calm, endearing expression that made her feel she could go on. In fact, when faced with those eyes, she wanted to tell him everything.

"My mother."

She said it very simply, without emotion or color. His expression never flinched or flickered. His hand reached for hers and she looked down. This time he took her hand in both of his, covering it with warmth and the slight roughness of maturity. Again she felt her heart beat fast, and the strange sensation of warmth seize her like a wick catching fire.

"Your mother's name was Anne Boleyn. She was mistress to the King and then wedded. Her status as Queen was not accepted by the majority of England. The King obtained a nullity from the Archbishop to sever his marriage to Queen Catherine of Aragon, mother of your sister Mary, whose title as Princess was stripped, and it was at this time that she was banished. Catherine refused the authority of the Archbishop, saying she would submit only to the decree of the Pope. King Henry fully intended to father his successor. He was disgraced with the birth of a daughter. The next year, the Pope officially favored Catherine in the matter of the King's polygamy, and at the same time Parliament passed the Act of Succession, ratifying Anne's position as Queen. In November, the breach with Rome was complete, and the Act of Supremacy declared King Henry to be Head of the Church in England, so that it became high treason to honor Catherine as Queen. The King turned his courting now to Jane Seymour, figuring how to bring her to the throne as the new Queen. Queen Catherine miscarried a son. The King had her arrested for adultery, the charge being made against her and her natural brother and four other men. Through torture, the only man to confess was her brother. Queen Catherine denied the charges, and was suspected of a complete collapse of nerves and reason at this point. Thomas Cramner granted the nullity on the seventeenth of May, thus establishing the King's paternity of yourself, and pronouncing you a maternal bastard. Queen Catherine was sentenced to die the next morning. The execution was delayed one day due to the late arrival of the executioner, who was imported from Calais, as he was the only English subject skilled to behead with a sword. On Friday the nineteen of May, at eight o'clock in the morning, she was killed, at twenty-nine years of age. She had reigned as Queen fourteen days short of three years. She greeted her death strangely cheerfully, still swearing to her fidelity. She was buried in the choir of St. Peter-ad-Vincula in the Tower. The next day King Henry and Jane Seymour were betrothed at Chelsea in Middlesex. They were wed on the thirtieth at Whitewall, and she took her place on the Queen's throne."

She listened the way she listened to everything, with complete absorption. Then she withdrew her hand and rose in ladylike fashion. He rose with her.

"Thank you. Thank you very much. You are a good friend to me."

He nodded slightly, appearing pleased that she behaved admirably. "Any time I may be of service to my young mistress.

I bid you good evening."

"Good evening."

She closed the door behind him, exhaling deeply and standing there a moment. Then she turned and called for Kat to draw a hot evening bath.

⁓

Life moved Elizabeth constantly from Hertfield to Enfield, Ashridge, Hatfield, Hunson, Havering Bower, to Hampton Court and finally Greenwich to visit her father. In each of these places, Elizabeth had her private chamber and sundry comforts to embrace with the comfort of recognition. Traveling in regal procession with her staff, she took in a good wide view of England and its varied inhabitants, along with their varied reactions to seeing this pretty young princess moving through their streets and past their own houses. She fell in love with the untouched countryside, the majestic fir trees and rolling green grasses. She looked straight into the faces of the rustic people who left their plows and axes to come to the roadside and wave to her, the gardeners turning from their flowers and bush firs and ivies, the city tradesmen and unshaven workers who shouted from the wharf, cheering to her health, the children who all looked younger than she, skipping home with their schoolbooks. The churches differed from town to town in size and decorum, some barely recognizable as towns save for the inevitable wooden cross. She knew she was a glittering spectacle to them as she passed through.

One day in the garden, surrounded by shiny holly leaves and rosemary, she told Kat, "It cheers them to see me. They should have a bigger show of it, for all their spirited hospitality."

"My lady's smile is all that is required for satisfaction."

She drew deeply of the clean air, the sky blue and bright. "They deserve more. These are my people, and I would be a proper figure for them."

Thus began her attention to her wardrobe, which

soon climbed out of Kat's control. Her young mistress was developing extravagant tendencies in her dress, and new seamstresses were brought into her company.

"You see, Kat, how well it does them, to have a star that glitters in the shadowy regions of politics. It taxes me not a whit to please them thus, and you see what a point of contrast I can provide."

She swept her arm out in an arc, indicating the ugly sight of the gallows on a nearby hill, one still dangling a withering corpse. The smell of sewage swelled in waves from village to village, and visible too was the occasional cripple, hobbling through the streets to beg his next meal. Against this she could shine, in her silver and white, the embroidered trim and numerous ribbons and bows. Larger, larger she sought the picture to be, and larger her image grew, the collars rising, ruffs thickening, sleeves puffing over layers and layers of undergarments, her tiny but undeniably womanly body becoming exquisitely accentuated through a thousand hooks and eyes, her shapely legs beneath all the pageantry clothed in silk stockings. Jewels became her and were sent to her in droves, all the finest work of gemcutters eagerly bequeathed to her. Her fine young face smiled with benevolence from ruby and emerald studded headdresses, the soft auburn hair continuing her radiance next to her skin. This was her present to them, her beloved people, to the England she looked on with all the pride that a mother can give to her children.

She knew not only how to emphasize her charms, but how to employ them. In her private world of the people she had about her daily were Kat, now Mrs. John Ashley, Edward, the close attendants and of course Grindal. She did not attempt to bedazzle them with the brilliance of her stage appearance. And yet the theatricality was there, in just the opposite way— her graceful offhand gestures, subtle looks and movements of her body, the slyly sensuous ways she moved her lips and her eyes. Men reacted to her, her strange mix of womanliness and her untouchable qualities of being regality and yet a child. More than this, though, she impressed her character upon people with her cutting wit and quickness of tongue. Her mind was her greatest asset, despite all her blossoming physical charms, and, when coupled with her knowledge of manners and sterling formal politeness, she was a formidable force of feminacy indeed.

Kat was keenly aware of the effect she had on men, perhaps almost painfully aware. She wanted desperately to guard her ward and keep her as unblemished as she had been the first day she'd seen her. She did not hesitate to scold male servants or visitors if she even suspected they had looked at her mistress inappropriately, and she stood vigilant as a gargoyle over Elizabeth in public. The part that promised to make all of this more difficult than Elizabeth's outright sensuality in itself was that Elizabeth was aware of her charms, and enjoyed the power of using them. Had this not been the case, perhaps Kat's job would have been easier. But as quickly as Elizabeth was blossoming, it was sure to happen any day that Elizabeth would not only be aware of the glances of men; she would return them.

Grindal worked the princess to the utmost of her ability, always treating it in the stride that such intensity was simply the way things were done. For long, concentrated hours they read Greek, or poured through the grammar of Italian, relentlessly contriving ideas into new words, forcing agreement of case, tense, and gender. Without respite they poured the next day into French, with relentless perfection of pronunciation. He was insistent on details; the French *l* of *ville* was not to sound like the English *l* of *pill*. The English word *veal* contained the correct sound, and they would repeat it tens of times until she got it right. A word ending in a consonant followed by a beginning vowel in the following word would lend its consonant to that next word, and so on. To speak was to speak correctly.

"To speak with an accent is to show an unwillingness to

learn, or even a deficiency of faculty. There is absolutely no excuse for a person to learn a language and not speak it as is should be spoken," Grindal instructed her. "Dialects are another matter. To speak in a dialect by right of upbringing is understandable. Ideally, a language should be spoken without a trace of formal speech. The learning of dialects is done for specific reasons such as to pass as a native or to flatter. We have no reason here to speak either with accent or dialect in any language we learn. To do so is inexplicable. It is an immediate poor reflection on oneself, an insult to the listener, and a perpetuation of incorrectness."

Young Elizabeth never complained of her workload. On the contrary, she embraced it, and sought to learn everything as completely and correctly as she possibly could. Kat made sure Grindal and Elizabeth had plenty of tea and no intrusions. In the mornings after prayer, Elizabeth and Edward continued their study together, sometimes sharing an exciting or puzzling prospect, but most generally simply sitting or lying side by side with their books, immersed in their own private brain fevers.

In July of 1543, her father had married Katherine Parr, who became the strongest force of a stepmother that Elizabeth had ever experienced, having seen stepmothers come and go like the changing of seasons. Katherine, though, took a natural liking to Elizabeth, and made a point of seeing to her welfare. Often she traveled solely to see Elizabeth, whereupon they would take tea and talk for hours, laughing and interrupting each other for excitement. She had a famously high concern for education as rule, and kept a careful eye over the lessons Elizabeth was learning.

One visit found Katherine gazing round the small room they studied in, surveying the quill pens and clean paper.

Grindal entered the chamber and bowed immediately to his knee.

"I beg your most humble pardon, your Highness. I had not thought you to be in the chamber."

Katherine's eyes glinted with the sight of Grindal. "Rise. I had wont to see the place in which Elizabeth studies. I had not wished to be announced." She drew her fingertips over the volume of Boethius that lay on the table. "You seem to do very well with her. She advances quickly, and possesses all she reads."

"This is due to herself. Hers is a keen mind that retains everything invited into it. It is an honor to teach such a one."

She smiled. "This is just the sort of thing she is without need of hearing. Were Elizabeth to know you so complimented her, she should swell as to not fit her crown. You must know she speaks very highly of you."

Grindal looked down. "I am humbled and honored, Your Majesty. I hope only to please."

The door opened, and the airy skirts of Elizabeth swept into the room. She looked from Grindal to Katherine.

"Are our studies to have audience today, teacher?" Her voice was heavily polite from a throat so slight. Katherine kissed her on the forehead. Grindal bowed again with her movement.

"No, my sweet. I leave you to your pursuits. Study well, and report to me all you've learned."

"Certainly."

Elizabeth and Grindal prepared for the lesson, arranging themselves into the positions which had become second nature to them. Elizabeth raised herself into her chair; Grindal opened a broad book. Katherine stood silently in the doorway, contemplating the two of them, the ease of their nearness, the maturity that flowed now in Elizabeth's movements, the intent focus her brown eyes gave to the books. Or was it, she wondered, to the comely man beside her?

Perhaps it was only from a light mention in the day's conversation, or a father's typical overprotection of his young daughter. But in the summer, King Henry found it necessary to write a reproof to Elizabeth for her affections for the tutor, and in regal melodramatic fashion, refused to see her. She was much pained by his apparent disfavor and confused as to his meaning. In France Henry labored through the siege of Bologne and wrote thus to Katherine: . . . For heretofore I have not dared to write to him. Wherefore I humbly pray your most Excellent Highness, that, when you write to his Majesty, you will condescend to recommend me to him, praying ever for his sweet benediction, and similarly entreating our Lord God to send him best success, and the obtaining of victory over his enemies, so that your Highness and I may, as soon as possible, rejoice together with him on his happy return.

≈

Katherine wrote a message to Elizabeth. It reached within the month. The message was that she had not to worry. His Highness had forgiven her his suspicions but she felt that she must mention, in all her affection, that Elizabeth might step lightly in the company of men much older than she and not of her class. She closed on a high note, saying that she would see Elizabeth anon, and that she was not to be distracted from her studies. The subject was closed.

Elizabeth continued to develop into an evocative intellectual female, her radiance encouraged by her enjoyment of life. She talked of the things that she enjoyed, often to Edward in the morning, and more extensively to Grindal. Edward became a flawlessly cultivated gentleman, his presence larger than his years. Elizabeth was a ravishing thirteen to Edward's cultured seven. He too progressed in his studies and greeted them with the same vigor that he saw his older sister attack hers with.

"Will there ever come a day when we shall know

everything, dear sister?"

She beamed and stroked his hair. "Never, Edward. And that is something we must never forget."

Katherine showed meticulous concern for Elizabeth and continued to revel in her company. Elizabeth returned Katherine's attention with genuine fondness, and so it was that as Katherine began to fall in love with a direly attractive charmer by the name of Tom Seymour, Henry's brother-in-law, she confided often to the young princess. It was Elizabeth who told her that she in fact was losing her heart to the man. This revelation astonished Katherine.

"Furthermore," Elizabeth told her, "you feel you cannot allow yourself this transgression because my father is unwell."

"If it were the case that I held such regard for this man, as you say I do, what an abomination such a blemish would be."

Henry suffered constantly from open ulcers on both legs, and his sheer girth had swelled to such grotesque proportions that he had to be carried about the palace on a chair. His condition had been steepening, as of late, and it was naturally a public subject of concern and vigilance.

"My dear Katherine, you have been kind to me," said Elizabeth, "and so I would honor you with my bald truth. You are a good soul, striving to improve all matters within your capacity. Your character is such that you cannot be malicious. The weakness of your character is just that which is considered a strength—you are true to yourself."

Katherine made a gesture of protest, but Elizabeth raised her hand.

"That this man has called up these things in you is not your doing. Such matters are never one's doing. Human beings are, at root, creatures driven by their hearts and their whims. To resist these callings is to embark on a struggle both dogged and perverse."

Katherine looked away. "Such romanticism is possible for the common woman, but not so for me."

Elizabeth's eyes flared in an odd light. "Therein lies your greatest flaw, that which will prove your downfall as a ruler. Know your eliteness and expect it to be treated accordingly. But behind all this you must know, you simply must know, that the only difference between you and that woman is your set of circumstances. Had Fate blinked, you could have been at the spinning wheel, and she on the throne. From this premise, you can operate with full understanding of every person you negotiate with, honor, conquer, whom you allow to take tea with you or who kisses your ring."

Katherine was silent.

"The next trick is this: you must do all in your power to convince the world this is exactly not the case."

Katherine remained silent for a long time, her face pained, her eyes dull under the weight of her thoughts.

"I love you, Elizabeth."

"And I you. Now I must take my leave. Remain in my chamber as long as you like. You will not be disturbed."

Elizabeth's lucidity and strength were soon to be challenged in the most poignant of ways. In November she and Edward were separated. In view of Henry's condition, Edward was dispatched to Hertford Castle, Elizabeth to Enfield. The night before their parting, Elizabeth stole into her brother's bedchamber, and there they lay the night through, locked tightly in each other's arms. They talked in whispers, vowing love to one another for eternity, regardless of what might come. Through tears, Edward laid his fingers on his sister's face, feeling her eyelids, her lashes, her nose and lips, as if to know them perfectly and preserve their imprint. She kissed his fingertips, promising him she would write often, and would keep their morning prayer and study in her own private embrace. She sang to him softly, stroking his hair till his breathing fell into the rhythm of sleep. The night wore long and silent after that, she blinking into the darkness. Unsure as to whether she had slept at all, in the morning Elizabeth crept back to her bedchamber and under the heavy coverlets, clutching them to her breast.

The next day, she walked into the study chamber, closed the door behind her, and when she turned around, Grindal was standing, looking at her, black eyes enormous in sympathy. His expression was so pervasive, so utterly consuming. She ran to him. His arms closed around her. All the tears and tightness gushed out of her like an undamned river. She clutched him near to push herself deeper into him, the comfort that was he, the protection that was he, the sanity, and everything that was in his eyes when she looked into them. The morning rose deep blue around the two figures, standing still, wrapped around each other in the small upstairs room.

Christmas the next month was bleak, Katherine being sent to Greenwich and the gravely ill Henry being attended to in Westminster. The dawning of 1547 was seen without celebration, and the month was merely waited out until on Friday, the 28th of January, news came. Edward Seymour, the Earl of Hertford, rode to Enfield with the blackest of messages. He brought with him Elizabeth's brother, and while they were quietly joyed to be reunited, they felt the imminence of tragedy like a looming storm cloud.

He told them together. Their father had passed into semi-consciousness around midnight the night before, and had died in the early hours of the morning. Exhausted, overwhelmed, sister and brother again locked into the embrace of consolation they had parted with, only this time, knowing with certainty that this would be the last time. Elizabeth hugged the new ten year-old King of England.

❧

Edward was absconded immediately to the Tower, as was custom, for safekeeping, and Elizabeth was moved to Katherine in Chelsea. On the 17th of February, Katherine named Tom Seymour Lord High Admiral, and secretly wedded him in May. Elizabeth's nearly absent older sister Mary wrote now to Elizabeth, appalled at the rash action of her father's widow and begging Elizabeth to leave the evil woman and live with her in Essex. Elizabeth talked of all this to Grindal and showed him the letters.

"And do you wish to leave?"

"Would you enjoy Essex?" She asked. He smiled.

"My wishes are not to matter. What is it my young mistress would have?"

She looked hard at his hands, speaking after a few moments of the chirps of blackbirds outside the window.

"We do well here. It gives me pleasure to be with Katherine, and I think the air here agrees with you." She looked him in the eye. "You must tell me of your preference. Surely you have one."

"I would be happy wherever my lady is happy." He chuckled lightly and turned to his books.

"Tell!"

He leaned in close to her face. "A man such as myself does not depend on his surroundings for his happiness. I have outgrown that now."

"But has there then never been a home to which you have affixed yourself and to which you return in your dreams?"

Something in her words jolted him, though the reaction was so soft only she would have detected it. He continued to look at the books, but his eyes were not focused on them.

"There was once a place . . . which I do hold in my heart . . . but it is of the past now. I remember well enough its peace." His eyes reflected a private musing that she had never seen in them before, and she thought that if she would allow him proper courtesy, she would look away, but she could not. She hesitated only a moment, and then her herself asked, "Was there . . . a woman in this land?"

Now he did look at her startled, and the corners of his eyes wrinkled in laughter. "A woman? Me? No, not ever." He laughed again. "How is it that you come to such a question? Come, mathematics calls you, a horizon of new wonders in the same numbers you have known all your life."

She opened the book, fixing her attention back onto the pages. They studied on diligently for hours, and then she retired to her chamber. No woman ever, she thought.

Kat adjusted her lady's comforts to the new living place, and fell in easily with Tom. In fact laughed more gayly than Elizabeth had ever known her to, when he chided her with some little jest. Elizabeth slept in an enormous bed of walnut, with thick curtains drawn over the posters.

There was much merriment with the honeymoon of the new family, and Kat was kept busy with supervision.

"How is it that your dress is a ruin?" her fourteen-year-old ward stood before her, flushed, exhilarated, having run up the stairs to her wardrobe and having been surprised to come face-to-face with Kat. Her dress hung on her in shambles, stripped into nothing but ribbons. She caught her breath.

"It was not my fault, Kat. It was Katherine and Tom! Katherine held me down and Tom cut it into a hundred pieces!"

The horseplay brought out a new side of Elizabeth, a buoyancy that had never before been seen. Kat was both concerned and glad to see her child finally showing signs of being one.

"He comes into my room in the morning," she told Grindal, "and tickles me until I squeal. Then Kat hears and rushes into the room and gives him such a stern look that he cannot but excuse himself and make off." Her eyes danced at the joke, and she waited for Grindal to laugh with her, but found that this time he did not share her humor.

"You may tell me these things, and I will be glad to hear them. But I tell you now, I do not condone his behavior. He is a grown man, and you are a young woman. He has no place about your bedchamber."

She immediately sobered, struck with this tone of disapproval she that had never heard before. She felt suddenly embarrassed without knowing why and turned without further adieu to the lesson.

But the antics did continue, Tom creeping into Elizabeth's bedchamber sometimes even before she awoke. He pulled her curtains opens, singing good morning, and lurched as if he would jump into the very bed with her. She would shriek and laugh, hiding herself deep into the bed so that he could not reach her. When she had risen, he would pass her in the hall and strike her on the buttocks or quickly run his hand down her back. Most of the household passed it off as horseplay, especially when Tom twice came into her room with Katherine, and they tickled Elizabeth in her bed until the tears came rolling down her cheeks. Once and only once did Elizabeth run and jump back into the bed when she heard Tom's approach in the presence of all her attending maidens. Kat seized upon Tom in the gallery afterward and scorned him hotly, saying, "There have been complaints of these things, and ill things have been said of my lady because of them." Tom was affronted, saying repeatedly that he meant no evil.

"I swear by God's precious soul that these words slander me," Tom practically wailed. I will myself make complaint of this to the Lord Protector."

Distressed, Kat sought out the Queen, who promised that she would see to it, and for a while after, the Queen accompanied Tom to Elizabeth's chamber. Eventually, the precaution grew tiresome, and she slept on, and again Tom came in his slippers and nightgown. Kat, however, had taken to waking Elizabeth earlier and earlier, so that by this time, she was usually dressed and immersed in her books. He was still reprimanded by the ever-vigilant governess, scolding him for coming to a young lady's chamber not yet dressed, to which he responded either with belligerent indignation or over-jovial laughter, according to his mood.

Elizabeth was shy to mention these things to Grindal after their initial exchange, but whenever she ventured even to the fringes of the statement, she found him consistently objurgate toward Tom's behavior.

One evening found Elizabeth in Kat's chamber. Kat was folding linens. They had been long in subdued conversation over this and that, and eventually, Kat brought up the subject of Tom.

"My lady must guard herself against impropriety. You have not experience in these matters as of yet, but as an old married woman, I can tell you that this is nothing of note. A thousand men would behave just so toward you, had they the opportunity. Forget not a moment how he flatters himself every time he escapes with such insolence. His behavior is inexcusably base."

"Grindal told me much the same," she said more to herself than aloud.

"And well he might," Kat moved her eyes with animation. "There is a world of difference between a man the likes of Tom and a gentleman such as Sir Grindal. You would never find him doing anything even remotely questionable. He has high regard for you, has Sir Grindal. He'll tell you the truth about men like Tom and their intentions. You just keep listening to what he says."

All of England was so tense with the passing of the throne to young Edward that the very air itself breathed relief at the prospect of a masque. A masque was the brightest of spectacles and this one was no different—bells ringing out its announcement, torches carrying its glitter throughout the halls of the palace. The moon rose on the spangle of countless jewels, curled satin ribbons, and rouged lips and cheeks. Music lit the night from the lute, the harp, the shalmes. Great casks of wine were opened, one after another, drunk in the chase of banquets of such color and richness that they were pageants unto themselves. Poetry was read, many and many a sonnet extolling the Queen, flutes played Celtic jigs, skits were performed and jesters ran about the marble floors, smattering humor and mimicry with their painted faces and wands of brass bells. Toasts were drunk to the health and preservation of the Queen, who delighted her attending public wildly with every joke she made and every word she uttered.

The young Elizabeth charmed everyone whom she came into contact with, striking in her confident poise and ever-ripening beauty. Her gown was a dazzling crimson and gold spectacle, many hours and many hands having gone into its production. Elizabeth had quite an eye for these things, and had directed much of its creation personally. She stood now unequalled in grandeur, her regally pale face suffused with the glow of her excitement and youth. Throughout the attentions of man after man, she kept watch all over the crowd, studying the trail of newcomers with specific purpose.

"You will come, won't you?" she had asked.

His thick lashes drew over his black eyes. "I am one rather to keep to my books in the evenings, or the wood," he answered. "I enjoy long walks to keep my mind clear."

She had gone on with the insistence of a child, until he laughed at her change in character.

"Perhaps, if my walk has ended, then I could drop by and see my lady in her dress."

The words struck her like a dagger.

"Do not mock me! I am not a child wishing to show off her fine clothes! I ask you because I would truly delight in your company."

He was instantly contrite. "I humbly apologize, my lady. I do not think you any such child." Calculation showed on his face. "If I take my walk before supper, then I could dine at the masque. Yes, I could come. Of course, I am honored by your wish for me to be present, and I will come, though it may be late."

Now she checked every movement at the arch to see if it was he.

It was the perfect picture of a party, a panorama of young tailored dandies playing to women with piles of curls and swells of finery, the older men with their longer hair gathering into lively discussions in various pockets of the crowd. A young man with coppery hair and a sprightly gait caught his eye on a delicate pale flower of a woman.

"What's your name?" He hollered. She turned away quickly. People would be looking at such an outburst. Her steps lit through the crowd until she could stop, well away from the main clusters of people, along the far wall. She looked up toward the stage. He was gone.

"Looking for me?" She whirled around to find his black eyes shining at her beneath his cocked velvet cap.

"For you." He held out a red rose. She turned round to flee again, but he was in front of her in a flash. "Truly, you must take it. It has no sunshine here, save that of the weak one in the sky, and it shall surely die, deprived of your radiance." He was on his left knee. Her cheeks burned so hot, it was certain to be noticed. Seeing no escape, she leaned in to him, skirts still lifted in her hands, ready for flight.

"See here. What do you mean by shaming me like this?"

He fell back onto his knee, clutching his heart. "Her voice! The most perfect bell, the hushed tones that only angels sing. Speak again, dear vision, and thrill this unworthy soul."

She froze. "You mock me!" This time, her leather boots glided across the floor faster than any dancer's ever could. She was more than halfway to the door when the hall suddenly filled with applause.

"The next performance is by the Queen's private court musicians, each the finest in all of England."

She waited. Queen Katherine smiled as the small band

of handsomely ornamented men looked to one another in solemn acknowledgement. The music began. She scanned the crowd, anxiously hoping she was safely delivered, but found him nowhere. Her hands held one another in reassurance. The music was very pleasant, the sound clear in the high walls and arches of the ballroom. The harp was of gold, its graceful curve seeming to rise with the reaches of the notes. And the lute. She blinked. It was he. He played the lute for the royal band! His fingers moved effortlessly, rippling the strings like the surface of a lake. The sound of the lute was distinct, its rhythm undeniably effective. She looked around her, wondering how many admiring eyes were fixed on the lute player. So many faces there were, all pale and powdered, each smiling their very best smiles all at once. His face had not been powdered, she remembered, her gaze trailing back to him. Each player was dignified, immersed in concentration, all humbly becoming shadows in the growing light of the music. He winked at her. She started, looking down then quickly up, knowing her cheeks were flushing again. But no one seemed to be taking any notice. He squinted cheerily at her. She did her best to give him a firm, private scowl. The piece ended, and again there was much applause. Then postures relaxed as the hired musicians resumed with their dance music.

"May I?" A tallish, soft-looking man held out his hand. She was startled, and then shook her head.

"No, no thank you." He smiled and walked on.

"A spinner, you say?" He was about ten feet away, with two women older than she. They fanned themselves prettily and laughed, seeing she had caught them talking of her.

"Yes, of import. Seems she's very nimble with her fingers." The women laughed again, staring unabashedly at her leather boots. He looked straight at her. "Such lovely fingers they are." She ran out under the great arch, through an overly slow opening passage of smiling ruffles and frill.

Once in the outer hall, she dodged desperately behind a

huge potted palm. She found it to be a cozy spot, this bench among trees. The marble corner promised her refuge for as long as she was quiet, and she folded her hands in her lap and remained so.

People passed through the hall in all manners of mood and purpose. She was enjoying listening to it all, the heated political discussions, fussing about the twist of this dress and that sleeve, flattery and seduction, messages of new book translations, arguments threatening divorce. She sat still and mused that she held a far better position than any of the people passing. She pushed her leathered toe so to lean forward and began to peep out between the leaves of the palms, glimpsing faces and hair. They were a parade, a preposterous parade, full of sapphires and alum and that was perhaps all. If even one person would pass inside looking anything but ridiculous, she would be grateful for the conversation.

A new set of boots echoed their cadence through the hall. She ducked back into her corner for a moment, and then slowly looked again through the green branches. Leather boots. Boots suitable for heavy walking, or stepping through the shelves of a library. Boots of a thinker, of one unconcerned for his appearance here. Boots of a scholar. The sound of the steps came closer. She saw the simple leggings, the velvet cape. She rushed out into the hall.

"William Grindal!"

He froze. His eyes opened wide. His lips moved, but no sound came. They embraced.

He pulled back and took her face in both hands.

"Lovely Angelica. Angelica, Angelica." He said it over and over, their black eyes locked into stares, tears forming in her eyes.

"Oh, William!" She cried again. They held fast in the middle of the hall, a few people walking by but taking no notice. One person did, however. Through the arch of the hall stood the form of a young woman in crimson and gold, her eyes fixed on their embrace.

Angelica's steps echoed down the long corridor to the spinning room. Her lantern reflected light from the kingdom's marble walls, still black with early morning. She opened the door and lit the room. Everywhere. Red. Red was all over her spinning wheel, her bench, the floor, the flax, the linen.

"Like them?"

The musician from the party sat perched in the long windowsill, dangling a single red rose from his hand, then dropping it with the rest. She started.

"How did you get in here? What do you mean by this?"

He sat upright, dramatically stunned, then dropped artfully to her feet in a swooping bow.

"What do I mean? What do I mean, she asks? Only that I am madly, wildly in love with you, that you forever possess my heart and soul in there, the palm of your lily white hand."

"I will have a guard remove you." She turned to the door.

"Remove me? No! To keep me from the light of your shining countenance is to deprive me of my life's very blood."

"Out!"

He scurried to the door. "I will go, I will. But until you grant me an evening, a simple walk in the country, I will plague you with a rose every morning until the very country is naked of their buds!" He stepped outside the doorway. "An evening, that is all. A walk to grant a chance for a lowly and foolish musician like myself. Adieu."

He disappeared. She looked round the room at the carpeting spill of roses, each tender stem carefully clipped. She sighed and went to the door to close it. His bright, copper hair poked round to her face.

"I'm quite harmless, you know."

"Out!"

He ran down the hall.

True to his word, every dawn brought a rose at her wheel. She never knew how he got in, and would sometimes set little traps to usurp him, but the sun's first light never missed the touch of a red petal. This kept on for many dozens worth of roses, until one evening as she left her task, the unmistakable sight of the short gown and cape waited outside the door. She closed the door behind her and moaned aloud at her visitor.

"No, wait! I come with the most grave of concerns. It occurs to me, and I must know the truth, this question that has given me the most unpleasant nights, so that I have come here, seeking an end to my misery which only you can give."

She looked at him evenly.

"Perhaps, I was wondering, perhaps you do not care for roses?"

She made to walk by him.

"No! Wait!" He followed alongside her, she facing straight ahead with lantern in hand. He turned in to her and skipped to keep her pace.

"It would never do to court my beloved with the wrong flower! Perhaps this has been my whole error in approach. Be this the case, say the word, and I shall scour the land to find the perfect bloom. Beyond the land! I'll cross the seas, leave for long years of determined travel, slay dragons and enemies and conquer savages to bring it to your feet."

She stopped at looked at him.

"Tell the secret." His eyes were suns of hope and cheer, gazing into hers with all the intent of watching the moon move round its orbit. She stared at him a long moment.

"What possesses you?"

"Madness, my beloved. The madness of true love."

"You know nothing of me! All I know of you is that you behave as an imbecile."

"I know you came here from an island that was destroyed. You spin flax for the kingdom, and you hate it. You abominate every thread that goes between your fingers because your mind hungers for so much more. You dream of books, and parchments, scrolls of knowledge that have been taken out of your reach. You speak foreign languages, you are endlessly fascinated with astronomy and fine art, you can cure or kill with the clip of an herb, you are tired of the talk of religion because there is no God or heaven or hell and you wish you were back home."

She was thunderstruck. The silence was so dense it might have collapsed all the palace. The color had gone from her face, and when she finally spoke, it was barely a whisper.

"How do you know those things?"

"Lucky guess." Pandemonium. "No, wait! I apologize. Really, I do." She slowed again. "I do. I know because I listen carefully and I watch everyone. I'm the fly on the wall, the cherubs in the tapestry. I put things together and I have tremendous instincts. I can tell things." He cocked his head. "I can tell you another thing. I can tell you that you find me infuriating, but a demon of a charmer."

She made a loud sound. He threw his hands up. "Okay, so that last one I went out on a limb. You would, I promise you, if you gave me one small chance."

Her color had come again, and it was red, but so many things were apparently racing round her mind, that it was impossible to know just why.

"One evening. That is all I ask. Condescend one weak glimmer in the darkness of an unrequited love." He was on his knee again, and looked up beneath his lashes. "Please."

She seemed to memorize the opposite wall, a long unbroken stare at the dark veins running through the smooth shining stone.

"Tomorrow," she said.

＠

He sat outside the doorway, the olive of his hose pulling over his bent knees. His chin rested on his arms, his feet drawn in front of him. When she emerged, it was in a modest caramel-colored wrap and leather boots that did not look as though they were fashioned in England. He rose in an instant.

"To your honor." He held out the inevitable red rose, his voice and manner anxiously formal. He moved his foot as if it did not quite fit into his shoe.

She received it, holding it with the lantern. They walked down the hall.

"I brought two horses. I thought you might like to go to the river, and I brought you a cape in case you catch a chill." Outside, he stood beside the horse in the attitude of assisting her mount, but she deflected his intentions. Against a twilight sky, they set off from the palace, the crisp evening air filling their lungs.

It was dark when they dismounted and tethered the horses to birch trees. The spot overlooked the water handsomely in the silver light of the moon. They walked to the edge of the grass, jutting over the placid mirror that reflected not ten feet below. The air was thick with the sounds of insects which would probably know nothing other than this beauty. He laid out a woolen blanket. They sat.

"My name is Robin," he said. "I come from a line of fairly bright people, all English, who, when they haven't been locksmithing and sewing shoes, have dabbled in music. My father wrote some very good pieces, and I write for the strings in the court. That's all there is to me. Besides that I love you."

She blinked at the water. He busied himself with his belt and produced a jug of wine wrapped in leather. "It's so red that it's purple. You'll love it." He unfastened a sack with two proper wine glasses and a loaf of bread.

"Thank you." She took the glass, he poured it nearly full, and they touched glasses.

"To our first night together." His voice was still most polite. "I don't know you."

"You know me," he answered. "You know everything

about me. I've just told it you. Besides, I'm completely harmless. Really."

The quiet set in again, but before it could get too far, he produced a lute.

"That's different from the one you played at the masque."

"This is my personal prize. It's been around longer than I have, and it has traveled over many a hill and dale." He played lightly, so lightly it seemed not to disturb the insects, nor the owls, and she set down her glass. She moved back a little so that her back could rest against the low trunk of an oak and sipped her wine again. She looked at him when she was sure he wasn't looking her way and studied his face, the arched thick brows, so dark under his extraordinary hair. It was all one length, and though he swept it back, as all young men did, it refused to obey and now as he nodded his head with the music, it toppled into his face. She laughed. He looked to her surprised, never ceasing playing, and then smiled and put his head back down. The music was sweet and light, seeming to belong here in these woods, she thought, ironic as the idea was. She closed her eyes and heard swallows through the trees, and somewhere far off the fall of water over shallow rapids.

᠆

They met this way every night for the next three dozen roses, she saying near to nothing and he blurting out outrageous sentences sounding more like poetry than conversation, and playing his lute, trying new music for her, singing her songs of her delicate beauty and fine voice. Each night he brought the flagon of wine, and eventually she uncovered from her skirts hunks of cheese and fruit.

One night found the moon enormous, trailing wisps of cloud across its reaching glow, the water sparkling with the soft kiss of the breeze. He had played exquisitely, simple voiceless music that carried out the stars and settled him into the roots of the oak. He laid the lute beside him.

"I come from an island named Daculi. The land I came from is a beautiful land, of many more trees than people. The mountains are higher than any that are here, the lakes bluer, and the flowers more fragrant. The winters are white, but we kept warm in front of large fireplaces made of stone. Our houses were simple, small, and private. Each person has his own. Even couples would keep their own private houses apart from one another. The center of our life was study. Central to the whole island was the sprawling place of study, where tutors taught their own students. We have no school classes like you do, where people are taught all together. One teacher may have many students, but they are each taught individually, in the utmost of privacy, without interruption, for whatever duration the lesson might be."

"Sometimes you say was, sometimes you say is," he said.

She looked down. "Forgive me that. I am bound to."

"Of course." He kissed her hand.

"While every scholar has a specialty, each is capable of teaching anything, as will each student, with maturity. We learn languages, both those that are in current use and those which are obscure or only written. We do import teachers for this. The only ways a person may come to the island are either as a scholar or a lover, the latter being a rare exception. Our people have lived so long together that there are enough of us to couple among ourselves, and we are generally more than compatible, so. But this is away from our studies. Besides languages, we study all of the arts, and master every technique we study before moving on to the next. Because of this, any person from Daculi could play any instrument, paint any tradition, write in any style of verse. Does this seem impressive to you? It should not. Any person can be taught to do many things. What one concentrates on, one does. The trick lies not in this at all, for it is only a result of study, but rather in that which cannot be taught, the inspiration. This is what distinguishes an artist from a master. The master can produce what is expected of him, while the artist creates that which is never dreamt of.

In addition to these attentions are of course the sciences and mathematics. We have made strides there, especially in the studies of the heavens, which have not yet been made here. This surprised me, when I learned this, but it would not now. And we have more fields of sciences." She was quiet.

"Are your people aware of a world outside their island?" he asked.

"Yes, certainly. We know of it, know its various histories and endeavors. But, you see, most have very little concern for this, or curiosity. The real matter of life lies in watching closely the earth and the heavens unfolding, and this is best done when the self is clear. Most here cannot be clear. They are forever needing to watch beside them, behind them, all around, because they never know what is about to happen. We always know what is to happen on Daculi. Life is always the same. We study with our tutors, we keep to the forest, sometimes to the discussion place, and sometimes we love. There is no cause to think of anything save what one desires to think of. But this can only be within a people who are of like natures and have similar ways of thinking. Everyone is different here. Some would not like such a life. People here are all of different pursuits, and some of these pursuits are, if I will not offend you, simply the greatest wastes of time. Fashion, goading one another, these things would make one of our people—unclear. We do not know of such things."

Her voice was firm on this last statement, and with it came silent, vital tears. He reached out and stroked her cheek. She continued.

"We do not give things importance which so often are in this world. Countries are always at odds here, pulling this one to conquer and that to collect more trades, to map more routes and traffic more peoples. And these other peoples would not be trafficked, given the choice, and then there is the question

31

of rank . . . and most of all, here people can generally study only one thing, and most often, this thing is a skill, and then must devote all of their lives to it in order to sustain . . . It is very different for me here. I do not like it as much. I would go back." Her eyes were filled with the sort of focus that the observer can never find the object of, although the eyes never waver. He looked at her a long time, and waited to see if she would say more, but she was done. The moon was high and yellow above them. He reached for her lightly and they held fast to one another, sinking into the grass to watch the moon through the trees.

᠅

Elizabeth took both Katherine's hands in her own.

"I'm sure it is nothing," she assured Katherine. "Probably a passing fancy, someone who smiled at him nicely, or batted her lashes while he was in a state of drunkenness."

Katherine's face was taut, showing signs of her age.

"Oh, my dear Elizabeth, you are so kind. But there are things you cannot yet know . . ." She peered deeply into the girl's eyes. "What did she look like?"

"Plain." She said with tartly. "She was completely without enhancements of any kind. Nature will not always be kind to such nakedness of the face. Her hair was long and sandy-colored, braided over her head and down her back. And her clothes, they were nothing but working class frocks. Her boots were strange. The picture of a washing-girl, or a keeper of the stables, perhaps."

"But how will I know?"

Elizabeth drew herself up. Her words were measured. "I will find her." Katherine looked at her, stunned. "I will search all of your kingdom if I must, opening doors and peering at faces, riding my horse through the fields, peeping in the stalls. I would do anything, dearest Katherine, for you."

She sobbed to catch her breath. "And when you find her,

what shall I do then?"

Elizabeth looked at her evenly. "Be rid of her."

Again tears streamed down Katherine's face. "My Elizabeth, you are so kind, so kind to me. I am forever in your debt."

She patted the Queen's ringed hand. "Think no more of it. I will begin my search tomorrow morning, and inform you personally the moment something surfaces."

Katherine hovered somewhere between despair and hope. Then she darkened and turned to her again.

"You say he embraced her as well?"

"She rushed at him, and Tom opened his arms and took her in completely.

Katherine looked away. Elizabeth stroked her hair.

"Do not be troubled, Katherine. These things happen. Tom is a just man like any other. I'm sure it is nothing."

$\approx$

Grindal was large in the small sitting chair. His curule fit him perfectly. His grace was flawless, despite the awkwardness of the situation, and Kat could not help but admire the quintessential gentleman that he was.

"I come to you because I think you are the closest to Elizabeth and exercise the most influence."

"But you, Sir Grindal, she certainly looks to you with respect. And admiration."

He blinked. "I had always thought that we had an understanding, a mutual allegiance. She has been known to confide in me, and I keep such matters in the strictest confidence, of course." He sighed almost inaudibly. "But whatever is troubling her this time, she refuses to speak of it with me, nor even admit to it. I have outright asked her more than once why she is cold, and that is all that I can do. I am not a man to cajole or scheme. If she does not answer my question, I abandon it. But her behavior causes me concern. She has been thus for a few weeks now."

Kat refilled his tea. "I thank you, Sir Grindal, for seeking my aid. My lady's state is my utmost concern, and I will certainly approach her on it. She need not know anything of our conversation."

He took his tea and looked mildly relieved. "Thank you, Mrs. Ashley. Your sensitivity is appreciated."

⁓

Elizabeth's search had begun. She strode regally through the halls of the palace, the shine of garnets winking with the swish of her dress. She turned into the washrooms, the chambers full of scribes who would rise, pens in hand, with her appearance at the door. The libraries knew the intent pace of her footsteps, and the women who scrubbed each bowed low at her curious scrutiny. The cooks and testers scrambled to be sure their pots were clean, and the very horses in their stables seemed taken back by their perfumed visitor. Her search went on for days, not only through Chelsea, but through Hanworth, Greenwich, Enfield, Hertfield, Hampton Court, and the Seymour Place, where they sometimes stayed, in London. Her determination remained steady through the many weeks, and never once did she flare in frustration.

Back at Chelsea, she strode again through its halls, which had known her tread many times before. She took no one with her, and carried her own lantern to light the way in the more removed reaches of the work chambers. The veining of the marble glinted smoothly in the flicker of her flame. She opened another door. An empty room of spinning wheels, evidently abandoned for the night. She held her lantern before her, so that the light spilled through the doorway. A figure moved from the back.

"Yes? Who's there?"

A shapeless silhouette moved toward her, having come from some corner reaches, a back chamber or closet. Now the lantern that came with the voice moved across the floor, familiarly averting the stacks of linens and piles of flax.

"Hello?"

The woman came around the wheels, the outline of her hair becoming clearer. When she turned, Elizabeth could see the form of a braid down her back.

"Oh! Princess!"

She instantly fell to her knees. Elizabeth looked down at her.

"Let me see your face." The woman was still a moment, then slowly turned her eyes up toward the Princess. Her face seemed larger than the room somehow; was it the light catching her eyes, or their ominous expression? She was examining her, scrutinizing every detail. She saw her stare move from her hair, to each of her eyes, to her mouth, and clothes.

"What is your name?"

The woman's voice was clear and high. "Angelica . . ." She paused. "Laem."

She continued her stare. "You will report to the Queen tomorrow morning. You will stay in my servants' quarters tonight."

With that, she turned her back and began walking to leave the hall. The woman rose quickly and followed behind her.

⋍

Elizabeth smiled as she entered the chamber. "Good morning, Grindal." She set down a small silver tray of sweet rolls.

"How's this? Are you now the domesticate of the house?"

She smoothed her russet skirts, taking her place beside him. "You have suspected rightly that I did not myself press the dough. But I did solicit their making. The recipe comes from the pastry artists of Vienna."

He gave a sideways smile and tried one. "Hmm. Fine they are indeed. Thank you." He finished the tiny cake in a bite.

"However pleasant the distraction, I will not be drawn from our studies, nonetheless. Today we first continue with our translation of Seneca."

Having been called to Greenwich, Katherine anticipated the chance to see Elizabeth without patience. It was not fair that she had kept the girl privy to this line of activity, and now having closed the problem, she had not had opportunity to inform her of it. She tended as quickly as possible to the routine matters of settling back into Chelsea, then sought the Princess out in her private chambers.

"The Queen is here to see you."

Elizabeth looked up from her evening needlework. "Send her in."

Katherine embraced her immediately. "My dear! I have so wanted to speak with you. Not yet have I had the opportunity to thank you for your admirable detecting and delivery of that harlot. No matter how many weeks have since passed, my gratitude is constantly springing fresh from my breast. Thank you, Elizabeth, thank you, as one woman to another."

Elizabeth drew back, smiling. "I am only glad to have served you. Now, won't you sit, and you can tell me all about it?"

Katherine talked amicably about how her suspicions about Tom's wandering eye had been confirmed by all of this, how everything fell so neatly into logic in her mind after Elizabeth had offered her this difficult truth.

"How so confirmed?" Elizabeth asked.

"No, my darling. There are some things you cannot understand until you have had more . . . time in life."

Nevertheless, she assured her, it was true, and Elizabeth had done her a great service by confiding in her what she had observed.

"And so, when you confronted her?"

"She denied it, of course. She claimed not to have seen the

High Lord Admiral that night, nor even to have ever made his acquaintance." Her eyes roamed over the pattern Elizabeth had been stitching. "But I was persistent. She admitted there had been an embrace that night."

Elizabeth sat up. "Yes?"

"But that it had been an old friend, not Tom at all."

"Hmm."

"Oh, she made quite a show of it, tears and all, with the most theatrical of imploring. She even claimed that she was with child from her betrothed, to be wedded in spring, which, for all I know, is true. No doubt she would be of the manner to be with child not four months after being in the arms of another."

"And was she to be wed?"

She nodded. "Yes, that was true enough. I held her over until it was confirmed. And in fact it was to one of my court musicians." She gave a little laugh.

"Did you know the boy?"

"No, of course not. The girl hadn't been in service long. Seems she was delivered from an island that was raided by the Inquisition."

"When? What island?"

"Oh . . . 1532. Draculi, I believe. Inbred savages. No one was supposed to have survived, only some sailor took a liking to her and harbored her to England, she claimed."

Elizabeth was quiet.

"The upshot of all this, of course, is that she is gone, Tom knows nothing of it all, and she will no longer trouble my kingdom."

Elizabeth nodded. "Naturally, then, you had her hanged."

Katherine smoothed her hair. "No, actually, I didn't see the reason to. Perhaps I had a moment of softness. I exiled her to Scotland. There she will surely be taken care of soon enough."

Elizabeth's face locked, all her tender features turned to stone. "What?" She said softly.

37

"She'll trouble me no more. And I do thank you, more than words can express. Anyway, I don't believe the affair could have been serious, especially if she were with child. And at thirty-one years of age! Goodness." Something strange was happening in the Princess's face, like the passing of a thousand shades of color, quick as the Aurora Borealis.

"Elizabeth dear, are you ill?" She set down her cup. "Do you feel well?"

The Princess rose up, all the might of her royal blood and the fire of her fourteen years flaring in her eyes.

"This is why you are a failure!" She shouted.

"Elizabeth?" Her eyes were wide.

"Are you so soft? Have you no spine, woman?" She snatched a vase from the table and hurled it against the wall, shattering it into a thousand pieces. "One simple task, so simple. Any nit could see that she should have been put to death!"

Katherine rose, uncomprehending and more than a little frightened. "Elizabeth? Come now, you needn't worry for me. She is far from Thomas's reach. The harsh Inquisition in Scotland—"

"You cannot rule England like this! England needs and deserves someone harder of resolution! Someone who will not quiver in the face of justice. My father, for all his mistakes, would never have wavered, not for a moment! Is it because you are a woman? Is that it? Is your very nature flawed?"

Katherine crossed quickly to the door and whirled around to face her. "This is either some overspill of concern gone awry in the quirky moods of the night, or it is the sign of imminent lunacy. I hope, dear Elizabeth, for all our sakes it comes clear when you wake. Good night!" The attendant showed her out.

⮑

Kat Ashley sat and crossed her hands in her lap.

"I do not know what to do. You are not the only one who has sought my intervention."

"Who then?" The Queen asked.

"Sir Grindal, Your Highness. He came to be troubled of her moods some fortnight ago, but he had returned to thank me only recently, saying her natural disposition had been restored. And in that time, I had done nothing, only try to coax her confidence, which she would not yield."

The Queen's rings glittered on her pale hand. "Well then, we must only watch and pray."

"This may be, for all we might expect, the young lady's change from girlhood into a woman. Such an age, with the pressures of the palace, perhaps all of these things have suddenly become real to her, and are running round her mind all of the time."

"Perhaps." The Queen smiled weakly.

"I will tell you this much, Your Majesty. My Lady eats as well as ever, and waters down her wine with temperance, is always the mornings at prayer, and seems at least briefly elated whenever she returns from her lessons."

The Queen rose, and with her did Kat. "Well then, I am sure it is only, as you say, natural, and we must endure it with the forbearance of a parent. After all, we are to her that much. Two mothers and Sir Grindal the scholar father, eh? I think you do marvelously with her."

Kat was properly humbled, and the Queen went to her duties of the day.

⁓

Everything seemed to settle back into normalcy. Elizabeth giggled at the antics of Tom, who kept them as invisible to Kat and Katherine as possible. In her studies, she progressed rapidly, soon fluently conversing with Grindal in French, Italian, Latin, and sometimes even requesting that they conduct other studies in these languages. Her tutor obliged, inwardly glowing with pride at the progress of his royal student.

A harsh England winter set in, with cold temperatures that did anything but daunt Elizabeth from pursuing life outdoors. She and Grindal spoke often of the exhilaration of an icy wind whipping through one's hair during a long snowy stretch down the countryside. Elizabeth adored hunting and riding, keeping to her horse for ten miles at a time. She danced for pleasure, in the high Italianesque style, lighting easily through a coranto in her privy chamber. Her embroidery achieved no small degree of fineness, and she early had taken to the practice of crafting her own gifts. That Christmas, she presented Grindal with an embroidered silk scarf, wrought carefully of her own hand, with poetry verses in all the romance languages, and curving pictures of pheasants, snakes, hearts and doves, all its Renaissance splendor studded with rubies, diamonds, emeralds and Baroque curls encrusted with gold. The scarf stretched longer than he, and while it was certainly the most extravagant thing he owned, his eyes showed her appreciation for all the thought and hours he knew her to have carefully devoted to it, rather than its overt value.

"My mistress is meticulous in her decisions of design. I will examine it long and hard to appreciate fully your thoughtfulness and skill."

She gingerly tousled his hair.

"This crimson here, it is the very color my mistress wore to the masque so long ago." Her hand dropped. He looked at her closely.

"Something has upset you in that. What is it?"

She faced the window, no sound coming. He crossed to her and took her shoulders in his hands. "This thing that upsets you now, it is the same thing which had upset you before. Why is it you will not speak to me of it?"

She was surprised how intent his voice was, as if this genuinely troubled him. His hands now dropped. He sighed and turned away. She faced him, or rather the fine lines of his masculine back straining beneath his jerkin.

"If you truly want to know, come to my chamber after dinner. But I warn you, you may afterward depart from me no longer affectionate."

He looked at her carefully.

"After dinner then."

He was shown into her chamber. Her attendants had been ordered far from their usual passage, so as to allow the Princess complete privacy. She wore the deepest scarlet silk that day, and now her reddish-gold hair shone softly in wavy tresses over her puffed shoulders. She walked over the rich rungs many times with the racing of her thoughts, her cheeks blushed with intensity.

"Shall we sit?" He asked finally.

She looked to him as if she were surprised suddenly at not being alone, and gratefully coalesced with him on the small cushioned sofa.

"Perhaps this would be easier if I instigated. You are troubled about something concerning the night of the masque?"

She nodded, and then caught her manners. "Yes."

"Something that happened?"

"Yes."

He leaned in. "Elizabeth, we are old friends—and I had flattered myself to think—good friends."

"Yes, indeed we are." She was emphatic.

"Then I will be personal with you. Did a boy make an advance to you that night?"

She looked startled. "No, I mean, I suppose, but nothing that troubles me now, nor then. No to your ground question."

His dark eyes scanned the chamber without seeing it. She could see that he did not know what else to say.

"You told me once . . ."

He was instantly attentive. "Go on."

"You told me . . . that there had never been a woman."

"A woman?" Now it was his turn to appear startled. "No, for me, no there has not. Does that trouble you? Did you want me to meet someone?"

"Ah, men," she muttered. She turned to him squarely. "Who then was that woman you embraced in the hall?"

He was utterly shocked. She was mildly amused at his complete astonishment.

"Why, I never thought," he said softly. Then his eyes crinkled handsomely with his smile. "Oh, my dear young scholar."

This sent a shock of pleasure through her, though she endeavored to remain stoic. He had never called her that before. He saw she was waiting for his explanation, and a curtain of dark thought drew over him. He looked at his hands, and then at her. He did this twice before answering. She waited.

"I was born on an island called Daculi. We were raided sixteen years ago, by a branch of the Inquisition. I managed to board a small boat, and set into the ocean just minutes before the entire island was engulfed in flames. They set fire to us, you see." He breathed. "They called us witches." His black eyes express so much more feeling than his tone ever does, she thought. "I integrated myself neatly into the academic world of England, established a new background with a reputable family history, and thought, and yet do think, myself fortunate to be where I am this day." He paused. "Until that night, I had thought myself to be the only survivor. When Angelica appeared, I was overwhelmed. It was like seeing the dead."

Elizabeth watched the emotion in his face. "And who was she to you, on Daculi?"

His eyebrows raised. "A scholar from the discussion-place, a lively mind devoted to astronomy. We were both young then. She must have been seventeen. We spoke together now and then."

"That was all?"

He seemed transported to the present. "Why, yes. I told you I have never had a woman. I tell you no lies, Elizabeth. I certainly do not." He considered her. "Is that all that was troubling you?"

She smoothed her skirt. "Yes, it had. My thoughts had not turned to it as of late, but there was a time it troubled me deeply. It must have been deeply, to have come back in such a fury with your mention."

"Oh, my sweet." He laid his hand over hers and clutched it with feeling. A surge went through her. The light of the chamber was dimmed, the curtains being drawn for privacy. Now she could see the line of his cheekbone and brow. Without thought, she took his other hand in her free grasp, and the sound of their breaths grew shorter and tentative. His eyes roamed over her face, her neck, her bosom, and her hair. The air seemed too thin to breathe, suddenly, and she felt her lips part. His dark eyes and lashes were very close to her now, the shaven skin she had never touched, the strong jaw, strong like his hands. He was at once innocent and intent, and the mixture charged through her like lightening. Her eyes closed and she felt his lips against hers, touching lightly and then drawing away. He was utter vulnerability now, precariously awaiting her response. The snake of a smile played on her mouth. She kissed him. This time their lips kept delicate hold together, exploring, caressing, growing in heat and eagerness as they pulled one another in.

Tom sauntered down the hall, keeping a watch over his shoulder. He swung his jeweled walking staff to his side, in rhythm to some song he sang wisps of quietly to himself. Elizabeth had outfoxed him, or so she thought, rising and beginning her lessons almost before the sun came up. Too, too early for study, he sang. He glanced in the garden. Empty benches, gardeners already tending the juniper and hawthorn hedges. The chapel was empty. And breakfast had already been taken. He began whistling softly, his gait jaunty and bright. He swung his staff in cadence, the diamonds glittering as it passed back and forth. The gallery window. He dropped low and fell silent, creeping below it with the furtiveness of a schoolboy. A broad grin broke across his face, and, placing all his fingertips upon the sill, he slowly rose up and peered through the window.

His face fell. There, in the early morning darkness, was Elizabeth, with her arms around the neck of her tutor.

⁓

Elizabeth was in tears.

"No, Kat, I swear it isn't so. Ask all of my maids. I was at my lesson, Kat!"

Kat had not seen her so since she was a very small child. She was touched. She reached out and stroked her face clean of tears, though they continued to come.

"There, now. I believe my Lady." She took the girl in her arms. "Do not cry so. I will protect you."

⁓

"She was wrapped around him like some harlot!" Tom stormed round the bed. "I tell you what I saw!"

Katherine put down her hair brush and looked at him through the mirror. "You are ranting. Kat will deal with it. I'm sure she already has."

"What did you tell her?"

She exhaled with the tried patience of a parent pacifying her child. "'My Lord Admiral looked in at the gallery window and saw my Lady Elizabeth cast her arms about a man's neck.' That is all that can be done for now. It is after midnight. If you ask me again, I shall refuse to answer."

He cocked his head violently toward the ceiling, as if it

understood. "And she said there was no man but Grindal."

Katherine stood up and put her hair behind her. "You understand it fully. Now, if you wish to recount it all any further, you will have to find a new audience. I am going to bed."

He stood staring at her for a moment, his expression telling her she was the maddest creature on earth. "Perhaps no one is concerned that this man is molesting my fifteen year-old stepdaughter. Perhaps the world simply thinks it is all right." He grabbed up his staff. "I do not think it is all right! I know what I saw, and if it takes me to rectify this, by the power of the Almighty, I will!"

With a bang and thundering stomps, he was gone. Katherine sighed into the pillows.

She woke with a start. Tom's hands were on her breasts.

"Get off!" She shoved him with sleepy arms.

"Katherine, my dearest, wake up, Katherine."

"Your breath stinks of drink. Get off."

He stood up and did a wobbling sort of jig, landing in a nearby chair. He was surprised to find himself suddenly sitting, then laughed aloud. He managed, with tremendous difficulty of dexterity, to light a candle on the table beside him. He drew his hand over his head slowly, dragging his hat off and then dropping both the hand and hat. Katherine sat up.

"What time is it?"

He grinned. "Time for a celebration, my lily, my tulip. Come, have congratulatory wine with me."

She adjusted her gown and hair, coming slightly more awake. "What, pray tell, have we to celebrate? What has happened in the short hours that I have been blessedly asleep?"

He was undaunted by this reproach, even unaware of it.

He held out a flagon to her now, which she ignored.

"If you must burst in at an unholy hour and disturb my sleep, have the decency to have a reason."

He chuckled lowly. "Oh, but I do, Your Highness. I do." He laughed and tried to focus on her. "Bid farewell to the problems of conduct concerning my Elizabeth." He squinted in a horrible smile. "They are no more!" He drank.

She was awake now. "What have you done?" She asked very slowly. "Did you disturb that fine man at this hour of the night? If I have to apologize for you again, I—"

He dropped the flagon, wine spilling across the floor. "Oh, yes, I disturbed him. We had words." He roared.

"She was on her feet. "Stop that laughing, you idiot! Speak to me. What have you done."

His eyes gleamed like a child who knew the greatest secret on earth. "You'll have to coax me," he teased.

"Enough! What have you done?"

He panted, his eyes growing sluggishly wide. He reached into his pocket and dangled something from his hand, a cat displaying its prey. She stepped in. It was Grindal's quill pen. "'Tis all there is."

She snatched the pen from him, examining it in the candlelight. It was covered in blood.

She started to scream then caught herself. She stared at him, her loose hair falling around her chin.

"Poof!" He cried and laughed again. He pulled his head back. "Best you behave nicely to me. I'll do the same to you."

She smacked him, and he slumped out of the chair onto the floor, drunkenly unconscious. She dropped the pen and hurried out of the bedchamber.

Kat's elderly eyes were swollen instantly with tears. She had cried out, but that was over with now. Katherine peered comfortingly into her face.

"I share your grief. The plague knows no class, nor rank, nor the dignity of a gentleman. I am sorry."

Kat sobbed into her handkerchief.

"I understand your mourning. But there is in that bedchamber one who is younger and will need your strength. I entrust her to your care."

Katherine kissed her and left.

⁓

Elizabeth was that afternoon sent to Cheshunt to live with Sir Anthony and Lady Denny.

⁓

In mid-summer, Elizabeth was given to great illness. The public was concerned at the absence of their young princess, who, when she appeared now, had a greyish pallor, and presumably had a chill, weighted under the greatest heaps of skirts and wraps. On the 30th of August, Katherine bore a child and was left seriously ill afterward. On the fifth of September, she died. She was buried in the chapel at Sudeley. On the sixth of September, Dr. Bill, one of the King's physicians, was sent to attend to Elizabeth. Elizabeth recovered slowly but steadily after his visit. The nature of Elizabeth's ailment was never revealed to the public. But one dark night a month later, Kat handed a trunk and a small squirming bundle to a boatman, who left toward Scotland and was never heard from again.

– 2 –

The Exile of Angelica Laem

Angelica pulled the needle through the cloth gently, letting the weave of the silk open around the intruding thread. The sleeves would need many more gathers for the shoulders to stand staunch the way Mrs. Wishart wore them. She certainly was the only woman Angelica knew of in Aberdeen to dress in such a luxurious manner. But it fitted her well, her kindly yet stately manner, her unquestionable authority. Anyway, Angelica crafted the stitches in such a way that only the two of them need ever know of the secret bolster, the bit of broadness that the tucks lent the otherwise narrow figure of the head of the Wishart household.

Mrs. Wishart had been so overwhelmingly kind, she thought, to take this stranger in, and large with child, no less. She helped with the sewing for all the family, Mr. Wishart, whom she rarely saw, Walter, the son, and stitched a bit for the young daughter Jane. She was not an official sewer, however; she was Mrs. Wishart's housegirl. But she was not treated in the manner that most housegirls were, for she had witnessed others in the more prominent households when accompanying Mrs. Wishart, and the general attitude of those wealthy enough to have servants in this day and age was that everyone, save their god, was beneath them, and servants were so low as to not even figure in that gauge. She was lucky, and she cherished her position in life, being treated more as a member of the clan than as a housegirl. The atmosphere in the Wishart house far friendlier than that in the palace, and more than all of that: the Wishart house had books.

Not many, as books were only beginning to become available, but Mr. Wishart saw books as an essential, and not a trip went by but that she didn't send some of the boys to unload more volumes from the wagon. He was having her carpenters build a library off the sitting room, and no one in the household was to reveal this to the public, for fear of thievery and suspicion. One of the carpenter's names was Jonathon. Jonathon was a young apprentice, skilled in the art of carpentry, another waif who had been adopted by Mrs. Wishart out of some poor conditions, but he had been here for some time, and his young body had fleshed out, molding as early as ten years of age (or so she approximated) into a distinctly muscular and masculine form. Angelica liked him; she had heard him singing to himself in the room as he sawed, and admired his quiet pleasure in his work.

Angelica was invited to do her evening embroidery in the sitting room, and took the lowest seat with her work, while Mrs. Wishart sat in a coffee chair with a book. Angelica was quietly impressed that Mrs. Wishart could read. Often hours would pass between them in silence. This evening, Mrs. Wishart looked up from the pages.

"Angelica, I have not said, but I wish you to know that

your child is invited to serve in my house."

"Thank you, Ma'am."

"Not at all."

Angelica continued her stitching.

"There is more."

She set the needle in her lap and looked at her mistress.

"If the child is male, I would like to have him taught to read. I like all of my male staff to possess this skill, and sometimes send them to school. Do you understand?"

"Yes, Ma'am. Thank you, Ma'am."

"Thank me? Indeed. You impress me. Not all mothers would want their boys raised with strange teaching from the master house."

"Not strange, Ma'am. Illiteracy in any person grieves me, not least of all any child of mine."

Now Mrs. Wishart set down her book.

"Is this such a strong view of yours? Where have you gotten it from?"

"It is my thinking, Ma'am."

"Did the father of your child read?"

Angelica winced, subtle though it was. Mrs. Wishart remained impassive and waited for her reply.

"He read, Ma'am."

Mrs. Wishart was quiet.

"Did your father?"

"Yes, Ma'am."

The gathered sleeves pulled as the thin shoulders inside them leaned forward. "Child, can you read?"

Angelica locked gaze with Mrs. Wishart, and for the first time, Mrs. Wishart saw a silvery glint in her black eyes.

⁓

"You take it away, you take this food and you eat it all, even that which you don't like. You are not the only one who eats."

50

The cook Rena looked at Angelica's large belly as she talked. She smiled gratefully and took the plate with both hands. Lots of meat, these days. She hoped the Rena knew how to account for all the meat she gave to her. But then Mrs. Wishart might already know. As she turned to walk out, a jaunty young form smiled up at her as he entered the room. She smiled slightly. She heard the Rena's voice.

"Can never get enough to fill your plate, were all the farms in Scotland to pour me their harvest. Sakes."

"Thank you, Rena. Can't have enough of your cooking."

Angelica was through the doorway when she heard Rena loudly exclaim. She stopped in the hall, startled, holding her plate.

"What a beautiful thing, Jonathon! Oh, such a lovely thing. You going to be a master carver, young man. Master carver. Oh, I ain't never had such a lovely thing."

Angelica continued to her quarters, hurrying to the new piece by Montaigne that Mrs. Wishart had given her, smiling and enjoying the hearty smell of the food.

The house always seemed to be busy, with servants shining and polishing, Jonathon hammering, Mrs. Wishart overseeing the house, Mr. Wishart and Walter stopping in only periodically from seeing to crop production and the wharf business, of which Angelica knew nothing and witnessed even less, and visitors were constantly arriving or leaving. Mrs. Wishart received callers in the sitting room, with a view to eventually using the library, once circumstances allowed. She had a conviction that not only would libraries be accepted and approved of as serious and valuable things, but eventually would be the norm to find in a proper citizen's home. This Scotch family and the servants of the house comprised Angelica's daily company, and she served them quietly and well, observing each individual carefully. She began to suspect that one of the family was observing her particularly carefully as well: Walter. Quiet stealings into other rooms and bowed head kept her hidden from him most times, and others she would become extremely intent on her stitching, switching from his garments to the little ones of Janet.

Janet, or Jane as she was known, was a solemn girl of perhaps three years, and she appeared even less frequently than her elder brother, ensconced almost perpetually in the nursery. Angelica had only seen her once, for her initial taking of measurements. Since then, she had sewn numerous articles for the girl but had never seen her wearing them. She remembered the meeting vividly, however; how strangely mature and elite the look had been in her small dark eyes, how somber her young nature. She wasn't sure whether she had been comfortable with the girl.

In fact, anything connected with the nursery seemed to hold an aversion for her. She tried to steer clear of it in her comings and goings about the great house, but nevertheless sometimes found herself outside the door, waiting for soiled towels or delivering a new nightdress and slippers. This was one such day, and the voices of the two older nurses carried through the wood.

"Bit young, don't you think?"

"Aye, bit young to trust to building walls and ceilings. Supposing you pass through in a rainstorm. All them books he's hidden rats and frogs behind'll come tumbling onto your head. Mark me."

Johnathon, Angelica thought. He was a competent builder, and serious about his work. She had seen him at work on the library.

"And what do you think of that new one, Lattie, the one with the long braid?"

She heard a grunt in response.

"What kind of trouble you think we got there, now? Must be due any day."

"Mind to keep her clear of the wharf men, come dinner."

They laughed. Angelica prickled.

The older one, Lattie, spoke again. "Why do you think the Missus has her sewing all these clothes for Miss Jane?"

There was a low whistle of understanding mixed with mockery. Lattie continued.

"Miss Jane ain't going to last in these clothes more than a few months. Then, who's going to be needing them? Mind what I say, I have an understanding of the Mrs. Wishart."

Angelica couldn't bear it any longer. Her hand paused behind the door, then she took a breath and forced it five times against the door. The women's voices ceased immediately, several steps clomped near, and the door opened to a lined and smiling face.

"Well now, Miss Angelica, what is it we can do for the likes of you?"

Angelica winced. "Mrs. Wishart sent me for the nightcap of Miss Jane, on which the seams show."

The woman nodded. "Hold on. Step in, step in."

"No thank you."

She raised her wiry eyebrows and turned into the room. In a moment, she handed the cap to Angelica. She thanked the woman and left without waiting for her response.

Her stomach grew. Soon all she could do was sit with her stitching. Mrs. Wishart seemed to be spending more evenings having Angelica in the room, and even had them both brought mulled wine once. After nine o'clock, if Mr. Wishart was not home, Mrs. Wishart would allow her to put away her sewing for the day and read with her. Angelica was humble in the special treatment and never complained of the illness that took her in the mornings and the pains that seized her odd times throughout the day. But she had the strongest intuition that Mrs. Wishart knew, and more than once after she'd frozen in a sudden pain, Mrs. Wishart would enter the room Angelica had been working in and bid her to sit and stitch while she read.

Then the day came when Angelica could not get out of

her bed. She raised halfway up, but her wrists trembled and she fell back from the effort. She breathed hard and looked at the beams of the ceiling. Marie, the older servant woman of the long wing of the house came to her.

"Angelica? Can you hear me?"

"Come in," her voice was faint.

Marie crossed straight to her bed and laid her hand on Angelica's face. "You won't be getting out of bed today, Angelica."

Marie's face seemed to grow hazy at the edges, the lines of her lashes and brows all merging into blurs like distant stars. Angelica's eyes opened and closed, and she felt the woman's hand on her belly. Then Mrs. Wishart herself was in her room, and she was sure she must be dreaming. All of the nurses were there, and she wished that Lattie would go away, with her pinched face. Then the great pain seized her again, the pain that shot all through her insides like a fierce raveling dragon, roaring its fire up through her loins and into her brain.

⁓

She sweated. She knew she'd been sweating for a while. Her clothes were soaked, and her eyes stung when she opened her eyes. She was still in the dream. Mrs. Wishart was talking to a man, and they were all in her little room. She closed her eyes to hear them better.

"She's come from a rotten man, that's all. She's nothing to do with our law here. Look at her; she's not even Scots. She's exotic. I can't even place it."

Mrs. Wishart's voice. She felt her hair sticking to her face and wondered at it not being braided. She murmured at this. The man spoke.

"The law is the law, Mrs. Wishart. There is nothing I can do."

"My husband will be here day after tomorrow. She is far too ill for any of this. Wait until then."

"I cannot wait, Ma'am. This is above me."

Mrs. Wishart sounded vexed. Angelica wasn't used to this tone in her voice. She wished she could have some water, but knew she was too far away to find any. She saw Robin's face. He was smiling at her, his coppery hair shining in the sun on the riverbank. She must tell him something, must tell him this secret. He nodded and listened. "The lessons," she said. Her voice was sluggish. She pushed the sound hard to make her words clear. "The lessons for my daughter are here." He looked uncomprehending. She struggled. "In my skirts." Oh, it was hard. "I've sewn them in. Teach her. They're for her." He smiled, and she knew he understood. She saw Daculi, with its tall green trees and heard the soft sounds of feet padding up and down the stone steps of the Hall of Books. The sky was so blue, bluer than anything here, she wanted to tell him, a blue that would carry you away. Play for me, on your lute, play your sweet music for me, and we will sleep in that blue.

-3-

Asria, Daughter of Elizabeth

The moon waxed and waned. The boatman followed the coast north and landed in Scotland. It was the pith of night, and his orders were, once he'd landed, to be out before dawn. He gathered up the tiny bundle in his arms and jumped down onto land.

Trees. Darkness. He could barely make out the craggy shore and mountains rising ominously before him. He picked his way carefully through the brush, the trunk sometimes catching on branches and jerking him backward. It made no sound. He was desperate to have this filthy mission over with, whatever the drama was in which he was playing this undoubtedly questionable part. He pushed up the steep incline, finally shelving the babe under one arm and using his free one to hoist himself from tree to tree. He was fortunate it was dry this night.

Hours later he saw the glimmer of a fireplace. What a welcome idea, he thought, the chill of the altitudes having bitten through his clothes long ago. He moved steadily on, breathing deeply and trying to make no noise. Sounds have such power in these still places, not like those of the city he loved. He would have to make good time to be back down to the boat by dawn. The faintest traces of light were beginning to show in the sky. The cabin was at last within reach, its stone form luminous in the darkness. He stepped very lightly, cursing each stiff twig that cracked underfoot. He waited until his panting had slowed and crept round to the front door. He set down the bundle, which was blessedly silent. Extraordinarily so, in fact. He pulled away the blankets with a sudden thought. No. Alive. He slid the trunk off of his back and lowered it beside the infant, settling first one side, then the next. He exhaled, his shoulders lowering with relief of all sorts. Dawn was undeniably nigh. He disappeared into the wood.

⧢

She grew strong. Her tiny limbs curved with miniature musculature, the tanned skin of her arms still soft with youth. Her hair streamed long and loose behind her as she explored the Highlands, climbing along kyles and sea lochs, her face moist with the morning mist which curtained the ridges of the hills. Her legs ran swiftly across the glens, bare feet lighting through the damp peat moss, carrying her to the enchanted inland shores that kept the most magical place of all: the woods and small green islands, dark with birch, fir, and narrow crests of pine. Here her arms reached steady and lifted her into the trees. Movement was easy for her among the branches, swinging from treetop to treetop over the moss and needles below. The sun thrilled her, the unfathomable light that warmed her and made the world alive to her eyes. She gazed endlessly at the patterns it made on her skin as it fell through the trees, moving her hand this way and that to see how it slid and speckled into shadows. She knew where to find cranberries and blackberries, and gathered them into her sack for when the sun was highest. Then she would take to the boundless stretches of heather that rolled like waves, and lie with her face to the sky, holding berries straight up in front of her and turning them in the light until the shine delighted her so that she laughed aloud, dropping them into her mouth.

The high north country knew the touch of her feet as well, the moors that the trees rarely reached, where herds of sheep grazed, so intent on their meal that they scarce heard her approach. She crept patiently, waiting low and motionless along the ground, holding breath and bursting in upon them. Then halloo! whoop! yoick! and the whiteness scattered in a hundred directions. She knew this land, this Scottish Highland, and her black eyes glinted as she stood facing over it, hands on hips, surveying the green-browns and greys that stretched uninterrupted for miles around.

She also knew to be indoors before nightfall. Papa told her often the stories of how, when the world became night, the little people all came out of their houses and filled the mountain. The faeries and sprites ruled the land now, and were she to visit the wood, which she must never do, she would be lost for all of its differences. They danced round the oldest trees in the night, glowed so brightly that their heels made sparks, and with these they made their little fires, round which they twirled in light-spirited song, hopping the oldest proper Scottish snap, which the humans had spied on long ago and still strove to recreate. Papa would light the stone fireplace and give to her the smallest glass of wine and water, and the moon would rise on their talk of the moors. The little people, he said, were here long before any man was born, and the mountain loved her laughing, impish children.

Tonight he sat her close to the fire and spoke with gravity.

"Your name is Asria, lovie, after the faery of the water. When men spy her, she turns the colors of the depths, and that way cannot be seen. She is a beautiful, strong nymph, and can pass through the world unsuspected. But she may be seen with the other faeries, come the most musical of their celebrations."

She was enthralled and was silent for several moments with pride at this new knowledge of her name. Then she spoke again, this time with yearning. "It sounds so pretty, Papa. Could we not sneak there one night and spy the faery dances?"

Here he looked stern. "No, my child. We who live above must never intrude on their world. The worlds of the day and of the night are very different. We must always respect their time, as they do ours. No matter how alluring their dance, one must never gaze upon it. Shut your eyes, child, shut your eyes tight if you ever find yourself before one. For many's the man who's been so entranced with the spectacle that he lingers and is bewitched. Such a man is never heard from again.

Her eyes were wide. "But why, Papa? What becomes of the man?"

But he only raised his curling brows and shook his head. "No, child. Never look upon the people of the wood. Some are not so good to strangers from the day."

He said no more that night on the faeries but kissed her forehead and piled the blankets on her thigh. Before he settled in on his bed across the room, she spoke again.

"Papa, if the people from down under become lost and comes the daylight, what should we do then?"

He blew out the candle. "You send them back to their houses, child. Tell them this is the day."

"Oh." They lay in the cabin's silence, each knowing the other was awake.

⸙

"Go home!" Her voice was firm. "This is the daytime now. You go home!"

The boy ran from her again. "I don't have to go anywhere

59

you tell me. Leave me alone!"

She picked up another pebble and threw it at him. "You go home. This isn't nighttime anymore."

He crouched against a rock and stared angrily at her. "If you don't leave me alone, I'm going to bludgeon you until your very eyes circumambulate!"

Her pursuit was undaunted. "You can't curse me. It won't work in the daytime. Go home now. Shoo!"

With a resolute culmination of all his might, the boy turned on his heel and ran as fast as he could, head bobbing and flushed red to escape. The girl with the black eyes stood staring after him, arms crossed before her. "That's right! Back to your house! There are hours until it's night again!"

She watched approvingly as his small figure disappeared over the hill.

$\backsim$

"Are you lost again?"

His head jerked up from the anthill he had been bent over. "Oh, no. Leave me alone, you bully! You nuisance! You dolt!"

She walked over to him slowly, craning her neck forward to examine his face. "Haven't you found your home yet? I have to send you back almost every day."

His lip began to puff out, and his chest rose and fell quickly. "If you vex me again, I'll get my father after you. Then you'll see."

She reached out tentatively and poked his arm. "Hey!" He cried. "I'm warning you!"

"Can you make your light glow in the day if you wanted to?"

He was clutching his arm as if to stop a bleeding wound. "You're crazy. You're a yahoo mountain woman, and you'll lose your teeth before you're thirty and mumble all the time."

"I told you, faery, you can't curse people in the daytime. It doesn't work."

"Faery? I am not a faery! You're a bugabaloo."

"Of course you're a faery. What do you think you are?"

He stood up in defiance. "I am an Irishman!"

"What's that? A kind of troll?"

"Don't you even know where Ireland is? Don't you know anything?"

She stepped in. "No, but you could tell me." Her voice dropped. "But don't tell anyone from the day world that you showed me though."

He twisted his brow and stared out over the rocks. "Do you really want to know?"

Her eyes lit. "Yes! Yes! Will you show me?"

He started to walk in the direction he always ran when he was looking for his house. "Show you. Yea, let's walk there. Don't you know anything?"

She sprang after him, moving in a kind of little dance at his side.

⁓

Deflation. "That's not the right kind of house. You can't live in there."

He kept walking. "All you ever do is irritate me. I don't why I'm even being nice to you."

The inside was just as disappointing: two beds, a table, a larger table, a fireplace, just like hers. He was busy hoisting out some large scroll, which was the first novelty she'd yet seen.

"Hey, maybe this is what's wrong. Maybe you need to make a proper house under the ground, and then you could be back with everybody and dance."

"You are strange." He pushed out the sides of the scroll, so that it unrolled, stretching from one end of the large table to the other. She blinked. It was like nothing she'd ever seen. "Now, this is where you are. And this is the Atlantic Ocean, and this is Ireland." He was pointing to and marks and lines that were tiny and fine. The cloth was covered with them. It was beautiful. "Can I come back and look at this tomorrow to?" she asked.

He looked at her doubtfully. "Yeah, I guess, but don't chase me again."

"Okay, but I do think you should live underground."

≈

"But what if I have to sneeze?"

"Ssh! You can't sneeze. You can't make any sound at all." The boy lowered the mess of wool over her. She held her hands in front of her face and squirmed lower into the bin. "Can you see me?"

"I can hear you. Quiet, I can see him up the hill." She lay still. In a few moments, the door opened.

"Hello, Father. Are you well today?"

A low male voice emitted a guttural sound. There was a shuffling of footsteps. The boy spoke again. "Would you like something to eat?"

"Why Thomas, if I didn't know you better, I'd think you were scheming something."

The voice was full and rich, not like the soft whimsical sound of her own papa. She liked it instantly.

"Scheming? Me, Father? No. No. Not at all."

"Well then, Tommie, let me put it to you another way. What can I do you for?"

Oh, Father, I was only hoping. I thought perhaps . . . "

"Out with it."

Do it! Now! Just jump in! She wondered if he was shorter than she too.

"I was wondering if you'd tell me about the cities again."

Small sound of laughter. Good like milk.

"Is that all? You want entertained? Cresseid and clarshocht! Very well, child. Pull yourself round the fire. We'll get it lighted, and I'll tell you about the city."

She didn't know how much time had passed. She didn't know when he'd started talking. She did know her leg was asleep, and she was having the most extraordinary experience she'd ever had. The worlds he named—she tried to remember them all—Ireland, England, Florence, Padua—she could see them, behind her closed eyes as he spoke. Her head swam with people with golden hair, wearing satin slippers and walking on flagstones, warm breads and cakes of all shapes and sizes, houses so high the highest bird could not reach their tops, little trees that unfolded color after color, colors bolder than the most perfect mountain sky. And the people of these worlds, all walking around with parchments and scrolls, speaking to one another in words no one else could ever understand, moving their white hands about with their speech, gazing into the heavens through a tube of thick glass. She didn't know what most of it meant; his words were even stranger than those of Thomas, but she loved hearing his voice and catching the hints of his pictures rising off his words like smoke. He talked on and on and she decided then and there that this storytelling was something she had to have, as much talk from him of these worlds and cities as she could possibly get.

The next day she was on their roof, staring down through the open doorway. Father was gone, and Thomas was sitting still at the table with a book spread out before him. She threw a stone at him.

"Cresseid! Don't do that!"

"What are you doing?" She dangled upside-down, her hair straight out in streams.

"I'm reading." He turned back toward the table and was silent. She swung a moment, looked at him, and dropped down to the ground.

"Is that something faeries do?"

"I am not a faery. Don't interrupt. Can't you see I'm concentrating?"

She walked around the room slowly, gazing up at a spider whose web ran precisely along a crack. She stretched up slowly toward the ceiling, thinking if she were only a little taller, she could jump and touch it, and then tried and refigured. Maybe a lot taller. She glanced at Tommie. He still sat, unmoving. She tiptoed up behind him.

"Faery . . ."

He cried out. "You are going to leave if you do anything else! I mean it!"

She put her hands behind her back. She could hear birds outside. She walked round the table opposite him and sat on the bench, putting her elbows on the table the way he did, carefully arranging her chin on her palms. She stared at him. Very slowly, he lifted his head. His voice was even.

"Why don't you get a book? They're in my Father's trunk."

He lowered his head again. In a few moments he looked back up. "Are you going to read?"

She adjusted her face so she looked just as he did. She made her voice flat. "I don't know how."

⁂

That's the end of it, he thought. I'm an orphan. He might as well have signed his father over, and said, "Take him; I don't need one anyway." He glanced up the hill. Even from here, he could tell what the scenario was inside. His former father had both of the chairs on one side of the table and his hands on the books, urging the long-haired girl next to him to stop pronouncing silent e's.

⁂

"You aren't to speak to them, lovie. You keep to your own side of the mountain."

"But why, Papa?"

He bent down so that they were eye-to-eye. "Those people hold the curse. They are tied forever to the people down under." He put his hands together so that his fingers interlocked in a row. "Linked. They have the curse. The little people can recognize one of them in the blackest of black nights. They traffic with faeries."

Asria shook her head, trying to clear it and organize what he was saying. "You mean they're witches, Papa?"

He stood straight, eyes wide and suddenly older. "Wherever learned you that word?"

She looked at the window, searching the sky beyond it for a suitable answer. He waited. "Where learned you that word?"

Silence. In an effort that visibly required all of his body, he turned himself away from her and worked at the pot over the fire. After a long moment, he came back and sat next to her.

"Not all witches, Lovie. But they all got the mark. They come from a land across the water, not part of this mountain at all. This is not their land. They come here to steal our land away from us, you see. They come in long boats, full of their people with axes and arrows. They would take over all of our mountains and have us wait on them hand and foot.

⟫

In the harsh mountain winters, she had to be especially careful, winding her tracks away in various curves from the cabin before she could set out for Robert's. Some days, the bitter wind whipped so ferociously that her tracks stayed not from one footstep to the next, and she grew so cold, she thought she would stop moving before she reached their fire. But her ruddy cheeks attested that to her strength, and she always went.

They studied poetry, Barbour's *The Bruce*, James I, Henrysoun ("Cresseid!" they cried aloud with each reading), and Blin Hary the Minstrel. She was proud to be a Scot. She progressed in numbers as well. Robert would set her to numbers while he taught Tommie, who was far advanced, but often she listened so hard to what they were saying that she forgot to finish her problems. Then they would switch again, and she could become lost in the verses. Now and then Tommie would tell her that she was doing well. Then she would become so exuberant that she'd grab him round with both arms and twirl him around the room.

"Father, would you please make her stop that!"

"Diana with a pen," he'd reply.

❧

The seasons passed, each bringing its own air and delight. Spring surged through her like the thrill of a forcible run, and she reveled in it, the ground breaking underfoot, the mirror on the water giving way to wriggling creatures underneath, the pervasive white washing away into potent greens and browns that swelled in answer to the sun.

This was the time when she could return to the treetops, and rush up the gentle slope to their cabin, where she would find Papa chopping wood or beginning a soup. But Papa wasn't coming out as quickly this year. Each day would grow warmer than the last and she would return from her lessons, sure to find his thin form outside, but even yet he wasn't there. So she would go inside, and he would be the same, pale, eyes closed, lying on the bed.

"Papa, won't you come outside with me and see our land all returned? We could walk down to the heather fields and guess how high it'll grow."

He turned to her, smiling faintly, his chest moving up and down. He didn't answer all at once.

"My child, you enjoy the land. I will be here when you return."

She knelt by him and touched his hand. It was so much smoother than it used to be, and her fingertips rubbed between the bones.

"I think, Papa, if you were to see the sun, and the blue sky, you might begin to feel better. Let me take you. I'll carry you."

He refused. She began to think of him while she was at study and wonder if she shouldn't go back to see him through the day. She mentioned it to Robert, who urged her to do so, and offered to see him if she would like. She looked at his Irish face and shook her head.

"Thank you but no. He doesn't get up anymore. I make him soup, and he goes to sleep. He says he is getting old."

She progressed in her studies, writing as well as reading. She could copy any poem they knew in admirable, precise hand. They composed letters and reports. Sometimes Robert composed poems and she read them aloud, which thrilled her to the bone. Tommie could write poems too; so eventually she simply set herself to it in the woods and brought it the next day as a gift.

"Cresseid! 'Tis a fine bit of work. You should be proud. Let's put this up in the cabin so we all can see."

She stared at it first thing every time she walked through the door. She began singing the poems they read and carried herself home with the tune, skipping over rocks in time with the beats. She shouted the lines toward the stone cabin, gaining in speed and volume till it was a run. Her voice cried high. She threw back the door and burst in a flourish into the room. She waited for a response.

Her eyes trailed down as she panted, from her raised arms and splayed fingers, through the line of her arched spine. She looked down and behind her, and over her planted feet.

"Papa?"

He laid still. His face and hands were very white.

"Papa?"

His eyes were straight little lines drawn tight across his face. She bent over him.

"Papa . . ."

The hair on her neck bristled. She stepped back, knocking into a pail. She turned and ran back down the hill.

Robert set down the bowls in front of Tommie and Asria. She stared at hers, and Tommie watched how the rising steam contorted her image. Robert nudged him, and he blinked, lifting more spoonfuls to his mouth. Robert spoke.

"Been down to the loch today. Saw a frog so large I had to walk backwards to get behind it."

"It's time we went fishing, Father. If we start salting them now, we won't have half as much to do at the end of summer."

"Fine idea, fine idea." They exchanged glances.

"Father, I would like to make a request. Might we hear some stories of Italy tonight? Tell us again about the painters there and also of the Flemish influx."

He nodded vigorously as he swallowed and gesticulated with his spoon. "The painters and the art, oh, the very streets shine with the magic on those brushes. I will tell you more."

They sat around the fireplace, which burned just enough to take the evening chill off and illuminate Robert's excited eyes as he spoke. Asria sat with her stomach half full of soup and looked at the fire.

"You wouldn't know whether a man had painted, or if the very chapel was full of flying angels. The colors are so sharp that your eye cannot be riveted to anything else, the light of the pigment clouds so bright that you look to your hands to see the shadow of the angel's wingtip. The cherubs are their little people, but they are rosy-cheeked and laugh when the slightest thing strikes them as funny. Their tiny wings flutter around the lady's legs, and their pudgy hands try to encompass the whole of a harp. It takes five of them to strum a string, and when they're through, on the other side of the arch, it is all they can do to turn to the next page of a gargantuan book."

"Do they like to read, Father?" Tommie was enthusiastic.

"Like to? Oh my soul, it's their life's pursuit. They know that all the secrets of the universe are all somewhere in pen and ink. That's why the little people all hoard books and steal them from humans whenever they can."

Asria turned to him, a lock of her hair falling with the movement.

"Every one of them; that's why they're in Rome, the home of all the manuscripts."

"Are there a lot of manuscripts, in Rome?"

The fire popped and its light glowed on Robert's face.

"In the studium called Padua I have told you of, there are so many books that they make the walls of a house five times taller than you and so wide that if you set out one day, the sun would set three times before you reached the other end."

Asria's eyes were large.

"They hold the secrets of things we don't even dream of, of the stars and the moon, and why it sometimes is full and sometimes an arc, of how the salamanders live under the water, and how to use your arithmetic to find your way over the sea. All the secrets are there, and those that haven't been put to pen yet are always being found out. The nut of knowledge has been cracked there, and there's more tree growing every day."

Her face had the trace of a smile now, and Tommie was glad to see a hint of color. Or maybe it was the fire.

⁓

Eventually, Asria began to notice that things were different this spring. They weren't cutting wood, wool wasn't piling up in the bin, and Robert wasn't always making sure the cabin was free of cracks after the snow. She watched it all carefully and finally began to be sad.

"Robert, next winter, we won't be here, will we?"

Robert looked at his boots shyly, as if taken off guard. "Well, now, Asria, I had thought to tell you one night when things were quiet, and we could all talk it over."

Her eyes were like glass. "But Robert, who will live here when we're gone, and what will it be like to die?"

"To die? Oh child, what is going through that active

mind of yours?"

She looked around helplessly. "We're going to die like Papa, and then no one will be here to see the sunset, and the cabins will just sit here, and—"

"Oh, Asria! There now, come here." He closed his arms round her. "The reason we won't be here is not because we're going to die." His face was bent level with hers. "We won't be here because we're going to live in the city."

Her face froze. She hiccupped in the silence. "Live . . . in the city?"

"Yes. You see, I have a wife there, and it is time that we be together again."

She was still too stunned to say anything. He looked at the ground, and then into her eyes again. "Asria, I got into a bit of trouble a while back and had to leave the city for these highlands, with Tommie. Tommie knows his mother and misses her very much. I do too. It's a bit complicated, but the time has come that we return and be together once more."

She began to look cognizant. "What city will we go to? What country?"

His face relaxed. "Italy. That's where she is. You are to stay with us for as long as you like, Asria. And after you've gotten a good look at the new world, the universities, the churches, the galleries and the alleyways, you can decide for yourself where you want to be. I have an idea that the answer you'd give me now will be altogether different than what you'll say a year from now."

"The city . . . will we see the books? And Padua? And Robert, when do we go?"

He put his hand on her shoulder. "We'll be here till the height of summer. Then we'll begin our journey. It'll take quite a time to reach Italy, mind you."

～

As summer wore on, she told all of the birds that she was

going and explained it to all the frogs. She talked in detail about the manuscripts she would be reading to the ants as they crawled over her arm. When she lay in bed at night, she wondered if the moon would look the same in Italy. She asked Tommie all the questions that she could think of and took careful note of anything he and Robert discussed about the journey. As the mist hung in the mornings, she tried to stare through it to its other end, thinking privately that if she just stared hard enough, perhaps she could see England. Then the ocean. Then all of her future.

The day came. Tommie had a pack. Robert had a larger pack. She emerged over the hill, carrying something over her head. They wondered to each other and waited till she reached the cabin. She tossed it to Tommie, who buckled and dropped it to the ground.

"That's my trunk."

Robert nodded concedingly. "What do you have in your trunk?"

"Don't know."

"Boulders," Tommie said flatly.

"It's my faery trunk. The faeries let me live till Papa found me in the morning, and the trunk was with me. They are the only ones who know what's inside."

"Well, now, shall we open and have a look?"

She threw her sitting weight onto it. "No! We can't do that! Only the faeries know!"

Tommie was clearly intrigued. "But you might encumber yourself needlessly. When else will you open it?"

Her hands were flat on the leather straps. "The faeries will tell me."

Tommie's mind was visibly manufacturing his next argument. Robert held up his hand.

"Good enough. That's between her and the faeries. Come on now."

He hoisted his pack onto his back. Robert and Asria followed suit. Their journey had begun.

-4-

The North Berwick Witches:
Ross Laem and Gilly Geillis Duncan

Jane Wishart had presence. Tall and straight, she carried about her an unquestionable dignity, making up in authority what she lacked in her mother's pleasantness. At twenty-five, she was fully the woman of the house, ordering the servants and directing the schedules, figuring out the profitability of the farm and the wharf business. She had her father's business sense and then some, which she used to run the entire house. Mr. Wishart was always home now, hidden behind a door in the far and richest section of the house. She told the servants that he was not to be disturbed, but a rumor leaked from the nurses of the Plague. Mrs. Wishart tended him night and day, and the servants occasionally made wistful mention of her absence about the house.

The character of the house was changing under Jane's powerful hand. She conducted her business meetings in the office proper, and very little of the rest of the house was used, as she never entertained, but the servants were required to maintain it with scrupulous care. The only books which came into the new library anymore were those that Mr. Wishart requested, and the rich mahogany moldings and petite rosewood reading tables remained deprived of the stroke of a hand.

The men would come and go. These were the same men who had come to meet with Mr. Wishart, or their business successors. Most were pleased with the fairness of dealings with Jane, but without exception all of them were displeased at having to deal with a woman, their displeasure ranging from disgruntlement to outright fury. Again and again regulars such as Alexander Thompson were seen to stomp down the walk, muttering about the abomination of being dealt with by a woman. She handled them all, sending them away in prompt efficiency, signing the documents allotting them straightforward arrangements with Wishart shipping. The business ran steadily under her, and at the end of their grumbles, the men had to admit that Aberdeen was aided by her smooth supervision of the port.

She didn't have use for most women or weak men. On the wharf sat a huge bundle of iron logs, welded together. The mass stood higher than most children, and served as their plaything on which to climb, until they were chased off by the men, in order to have it serve its real purpose. Under the small, severe eyes of Miss Jane, the wind whipping her skirts about her, a prospective worker would grip his hands tightly beneath its black cylinders, squatting low and with a summon of all his might, give a hearty push. The gathered men would shout Ho! and watch intently, betting on whether the man would get it into the air. If he did, he was hired, if not, with luck, the huge mass would be intercepted by a swarm of the able-bodied men. The dock bore the scars of those who had not been so fortunate.

Hence, it was not only a source of fair wages to work for Miss Jane, it was a mark of honor, and the hulking mass of her men bore their legacy with all the largeness that their appearance purported. The fields of the private Wishart farm and the house itself were filled with these men as well. Those of lesser stature and strength were set to their own devices or dealt to employers elsewhere in Scotland, regardless of their faithfulness or length of time in service. The men served Miss Jane with a cheerful devotion, knowing it was she who awarded them their growing image and fame throughout the coast. Among her leaders were Bruce, whose familiar bellow rolled orders up and down the wharf every day save the Lord's day, Buggerlugs, a tanned man with a swollen sideways face bordered by enormous cauliflower ears who ran the workers of the fields, and Rochie, the most colossal and ugly of them all, who was a stride behind Miss Jane at all times, her formidable shadow was known throughout all of Aberdeen.

Those women who served in women's jobs remained, the seamstresses, the housegirls, the nurses and the like. But if they could be replaced by Miss Jane's army, they were. Rena murmured often that she was constructing alternative plans in her mind, fearing each day might bring her replacement. Johnathon remained as carpenter, his body sculptured finely from his years of devotion, not massive, but obviously strong. Miss Jane ceased construction on the house, the library finished, and the H formation of the house complete, but Johnathon quietly kept himself constantly busy in his shack behind the house.

The housegirls who remained either had perpetual duty or they had none at all. Those who had none could use their time as they wished, if they were wise enough. Gilly Geillis Duncan and Angelica's daughter Ross Laem were two such girls. Both were contemporaries of Miss Jane, only a few years younger, and thus they tried to stay as clear from her as possible. Gilly said this would be best, as Miss Jane might take a dislike to them on principle, and Gilly usually knew about such things. Gilly seemed to know everything about people and the way the house was run, who was in Dutch here and in favor there. She knew what each of the Wisharts were like, even the distant members of the clan whom Ross had only heard mentioned. Ross had rarely seen Mrs. Wishart, for example, but Gilly used to bring her breakfast and told Ross stories of how pleasant she smelled, how smooth and light the fabrics of her dress were, and that she was especially nice to children, and made sure that even the lowest workers of the house had warm beds and enough to eat. She said they were very lucky to work for a person like Mrs. Wishart. But Gilly's face darkened a bit whenever Ross asked her about Mrs. Wishart's daughter, Miss Jane.

"She's mean," Gilly said in the safety of the woods. "She knows how to run a business better than any man in Aberdeen, and they know it, but the farther away we stay from her, the better."

Ross was fascinated by Gilly's worldliness, and listened hard to everything she said. The two of them spent all of their days together, attending Mr. Knox's church with perfect somber silence, and running off afterward to laugh at the image of their local preacher, the veins on his neck popping out with his high-strung voice, eyes bulged like the balled fists that he waved with his angry words.

"He wants to be like Mr. Knox," Gilly said, characteristically knowledgeable. "All of the preachers nowadays think they have to outshout each other to be real preachers. If you're a quiet man, better for you to be a carpenter."

They hid in the crevices of the wharves, watching the strong bodies of the men lifting cargo onto the Wishart docks.

"These are our men," Gilly told her. "They will make us

solid and impenetrable."

"What do you mean?" Ross asked.

Gilly explained matter-of-factly, never sounding the superior for all of Ross' naiveté. "What Miss Jane is doing is protecting the whole Wishart clan. The world is so dangerous now that one can be put to death in the blink of an eye. Remember last month that woman in North Berwick was sentenced for wearing an extravagant hat. If we were caught in the woods, Ross, we'd be put to death for consorting with witches, you can bet me."

Ross' eyes widened. "I didn't realize—"

"Oh, yeah, well, that's just the way it is," Gilly said casually. "So what Miss Jane is doing is insuring the whole business, setting it up so that it can outlive the legal system. How many clans do you know stay rich nowadays?"

Ross was silent.

"Exactly." Gilly nodded. "That's because the system is set up that the law takes all the money and possessions of an accused witch. So nobody holds onto anything. But the Wisharts will. The best thing we can do is stay as buried in her regime as possible. I'll tell you another thing." Her voice dropped to the tone of true importance. Ross leaned in. "There are other men in the clan besides Mr. Wishart. When he dies, it won't just be left up to Miss Jane to carry on the line. There are cousins, and uncles, and husbands and wives out there, all the way into central Scotland. Best thing in the world that could happen to us is to find a Wishart man and marry him. That would set you up for life. It wouldn't do it just yet though; bet you anything that Miss Jane has it set up so they can't touch the money or this branch of the wharf. She's gathering all of this power under her thumb so that she can direct it where she wants it, when the time comes."

Her words were sinking into Ross. She considered it all for a moment, and spoke.

"But where does she want it to go? When she dies, I mean?"

Deep in her thoughts, Gilly didn't respond at once. "I don't know yet. But she isn't greedy. I think she just wants to insure the clan's prosperity, to tell you the truth. But watch her. Whatever she's doing, she's good, and we can learn a lot from her."

Ross kept a good eye on Miss Jane. But she never seemed to pick up the vital clues that she expected to come clear to her eyes, enlightened as they were by Gilly's words. Miss Jane was just Miss Jane; she walked and talked and ate like any other person. If she did anything mysterious, Rochie more than likely saw to it that she was never observed doing it.

Gilly and Ross passed through the back fields to get to the woods. The road ran along the front of the house so this route kept them hidden. Ross was scared to death that if she was cited by any of the townspeople, she'd be instantly hauled into their wagon and onto jail, and kept close to the wood as possible. Breakfast had ended, and they hurried through the long grasses that broached the trees.

"Did you see him?" Gilly whispered almost loudly enough to equal a shout. Ross replied quietly to shush her, but Gilly never picked up the hint.

"Yes; wait'll we get to the wood."

Gilly's face was flushed as they ran.

"He never saw us once. That was Mrs. Wishart by the door. Did you see that she wears those fancy blouses?"

"Yes; please wait, Gilly, do!"

She swallowed her excitement and sped far ahead of Ross. Ross gathered her strength and shot past her, well into the wood to their spot. The fir trees stretched high on all sides of them, the oldest dropping off enough low branches to create caves to shelter the girls. These were hearty places. They had lasted in these hollows through rainstorms and crouched down on the carpets of needles and stray leaves. A chipmunk streaked away from the sudden landing of giants. They panted and sprawled out in their hovel. Gilly spoke.

"That window was supposed to be patrolled by Snipe's crew. That was pure luck we got to spy in."

Ross' face dropped. "You said they were on an errand to the city!"

Gilly shrugged. "Maybe they were."

The birds overhead linked the designs of the trees, crossing from one direction to the next.

"They know each other, those birds, even if they don't always acknowledge one another." Gilly said.

"Like people, aren't they?" Ross joined. "People pass on the street all the time, but they don't always look into others' faces."

"I would like to know the names of all those birds. I bet you they all live differently."

"Well, it can't be that differently," Ross answered. "They are all birds, after all."

Gilly rolled over and faced her. "We have to be back before evening."

"Why?" Ross refused to match her position. She knew perfect comfort on her back, staring up through the trees. Gilly looked off through the woods.

"Mrs. Wishart wants to see you."

Ross's head swerved to see Gilly. "What?"

She kept staring through the woods, her voice unfettered by the stark shock value of what she was saying. "Yeah, she wants to talk to you tonight. You're to meet her in the library."

Ross sat up. "Well, why?"

"I don't know." She rolled back onto her back. Ross sat upright.

"Don't you have any idea?"

"Nope. You'll tell me though, I daresay, once you know."

Ross thought. "Well, maybe I won't. You could have told me this whenever you found out. I could be going to jail. I might be being replaced or sent to England. Why didn't you tell me?" She wagged her head. "No, I will not tell you. You'll have to find out for yourself."

Gilly stayed staring up at the sky. "You'll tell me."

"Why should I?" Ross demanded. Gilly smiled, spoiling her effort to remain as indifferent as possible.

"Because I know the name of the carpenter in the back shed, and you don't. And if I don't tell you, you'll have to find out for yourself."

Ross was silent. She stayed sitting for several minutes, the mind behind her black eyes working intensely. Then she stiffly laid down beside Gilly, folding her hands over her stomach.

≈

Mrs. Wishart was indeed kindly. Ross liked her instantly. She was smaller than Miss Jane, her older skin showing the whiteness of her thin bones beneath. Ross liked her smile, and the way her face folded with it every time, as if it knew exactly what to do. Mrs. Wishart walked through the library, fingering the spines of the books with a gentleness one gives to feathers, and Ross sat very straight, waiting for her to speak.

"My dear," she began. Ross had never heard this term before, but it sounded nice coming from Mrs. Wishart.

"What is it you do around this house?"

She felt her stomach sink. She knew this was probably her last day in the Wishart household. She opened her mouth to answer, but nothing came. She snapped it shut and tried again.

"Well, Ma'am, I don't get in anybody's way." She stopped, feeling completely idiotic. Mrs. Wishart was smiling.

"What do you like to do, Ross?" She did have beautiful blouses. She wondered briefly if the sleeves weren't tucked up a bit.

"I don't know, Ma'am. I like the woods. And I like the ocean."

"Sea," Mrs. Wishart corrected.

Ross blinked. "Sea," she repeated lightly.

"Your duties are about to change."

The air suddenly felt thin. Her eyes were glued on the

kind mature woman with the pale blue eyes. She sat in front of Ross, in a high carved chair that shined in the light. Ross felt herself draw back slightly, despite herself. Mrs. Wishart was the perfect picture of composure.

"You are to keep a knowledge," she spoke in the measured time of vital speech, the sort of speech one would not think of interrupting, no matter how long it took.

"You are to keep a very specific knowledge that until you, no one here has known, and unless you pass it on to those whom you choose, no one else will know. Do you understand this?"

Ross moved her head up and down in fascination, then caught herself. "Yes, Ma'am."

That smile again. Ross nearly forgot herself and smiled back.

"Your mother was a very impressive woman. She used her mind. She knew how to read and write."

Each word that Mrs. Wishart spoke was sacred; Ross now realized that Mrs. Wishart held perhaps even more knowledge than Gilly. The mystery of her mother had never been mentioned by anyone, and now here was this blue-eyed lady who was speaking as if she'd known her. Ross tried to suppress her excitement to capture all of Mrs. Wishart's words.

"I am in my forties now, and my husband is not well. I cannot teach you to read." Her voice sounded regretful. "But the lessons your mother left to you will be passed on to you." She gave Ross the sort of look that was usually reserved for older people. Ross felt honored. "Your mother kept a record of the curative and harmful effects of plants. She said that this knowledge was to be passed on to you. I will rely on your inheritance of your mother's fine mind, and your cleverness of evasion in this house—" Ross felt her heart thump hard in her chest. Mrs. Wishart seemed not to notice. "Indicate their mental capabilities. Scholars of Universities such as Bologna and Padua are made to memorize and retain thousands upon thousands of bits of knowledge. So too were the druids in the old Celtic ways; none of their secrets were written at all. A good mind can learn countless things. Therefore, every Monday evening until you have them learned, you will meet me in this library after supper, and I will read to you these lessons." Ross was silent and thunderstruck with the magnitude of what was happening to her. Mrs. Wishart smiled at her. "You have your mother's beautiful intelligent black eyes. I know you will do her well." She rose, and Ross quickly followed suit. "I will see you here on Monday evening." She turned to leave.

Ross tried to remember what to say. "Thank you Ma'am. I will, Ma'am. Good day, Ma'am."

Mrs. Wishart paused in the doorway, turned, and gave Ross a very broad smile.

⟜

Ross felt marvelous. This kindly lady who for so long had run the household of the Wisharts was entrusting her with secret knowledge. She wondered if Miss Jane knew. Then she wondered if the servants knew. Looking about her with a prickling sensation of importance, she tried to detect any change of manner in the people she knew. Rena didn't know. Rena still heaped her plate with salted fish and bread, telling her to it all "like tomorrow ain't never going to come." The nurses might; they seemed to emit some air of knowing, but then they always had. She bore her radiant secret with a tall carriage, and brushed her hair with zest. Of course there was one nagging matter which would not be ignored.

"You can't expect me to just wonder for the rest of my life."

Ross had never seen Gilly in such a state. She enjoyed it in some wicked way, the relentless curiosity and the constant questioning. Ross had never had a secret.

Listening to Mrs. Wishart was sheer heaven. She would go over things and over things, repeating tirelessly until Ross had a hold on them. And Ross found the learning easy; she heard the words in her head throughout the day, while at the stream, or in bed at night. Even as she awoke, the lessons of the leaves were whispering round her mind. Mrs. Wishart had the actual pages which her mother had written on, all bound up like the finest books in the library, but with a paper different from any of those. There were pictures too, detailed and intricately real drawings of each of the plants she described. These left an indelible imprint on Ross; she could shut her eyes and see them again perfectly. Some were plants she knew right outside the house in the wood where she and Gilly played. Some were from distant countries, Mrs. Wishart telling her that these were plants she might never see. Now and then, Mrs. Wishart would exclaim "Oh my! Here's one I have never even heard of." Then it was all Ross could do to stay seated in her chair and wait for her to turn the book so she could see the novelty. She learned the names of catnip and chamomile, comfrey and feverfew. She sang in her mind long and pretty words like nepeta, origanum and woodruff, imagining the shape of lemon balm and woad. She knew that these were herbs, herbs which could live the winter through, and that others like myrtle, basil and rosemary were more delicate in constitution and needed spring's warmth.

Then the lessons became really magical. Her mother left a litany of secrets, too many to learn in two months of Mondays. She wrote how raspberry affected the pelvic girdle and cleansed the insides, to be given to expectant mothers, three parts raspberry, one part feverfew. She wrote that strange natives planted cedar trees on the burial site of loved ones to point their souls to heaven. She wrote the instructions for "plasters" to lay on a splinter or a wound, to draw out poison or to stop bleeding, or to bind two torn flaps of skin. Ross soon realized the gravity of what Mrs. Wishart was teaching her. These were invaluable secrets.

Then came lessons of harmful plants, the stunting influences of dwarf elder, the daisy, and knotgrass, how cyclamen could cause a stomach to upturn or even worse, how the fungus that grows on rye bread would cause the blood tunnels in the fingers or the toes to squeeze so tightly that gangrene grew. Ross listened wide-eyed as Mrs. Wishart's tender voice read to her how Helleborne, if eaten in small doses over a long period of time, would stave off the appetite until the person starved to death. On and on the lessons went, each Monday night a thrill of secrets and study.

Gilly was sullen. But she had resigned herself, finally, to being respectful of Ross' privacy, seeing at the same time that she had no choice. Ross was luckier than she, being given this attention, luckier and prettier by far, with her black eyes and the coppery glints in her brown hair. Gilly turned her Monday night attentions elsewhere.

"She talks about you." Gilly wagged her feet beneath her as she sat on the long wooden table. Johnathon went on carrying this board and that across the floor, working as though her words were mere incidentals in his lantern-guided work.

"How could she talk about me? She's never even seen me."

"Oh, yes she has," Gilly nodded emphatically. "She's seen you plenty of times outside your shed, working on your work. We've even spied on you. Her idea."

His hazel eyes regarded her doubtfully.

"Well, it was. She likes the way your back looks when you spread out your arms."

He looked at her sharply. "Somehow I don't think Miss Ross would speak the way you do."

She cocked her head nonchalantly. "No, I don't suppose she would. She'd not as wild and carefree as I am. I say outright that I like the way your back looks, and your legs too." She jumped off the table and sauntered toward him. "Anyway, she's no "Miss Ross." She's just Ross. Ross wouldn't dream of asking a boy to kiss, whereas I . . ." Her steps came closer to him. He clutched her arms and lifted her into the air, turning and setting her in the doorway.

"Maybe she wouldn't. And that, Gilly, is just exactly why I'd be prone to call her "Miss.""

Gilly gave a loud "humph" and turned out the door.

⁓

"It's a sacred knowledge, Gilly, given to me by my mother."

"Your mother? How do you know that?" Gilly's eyes were riveted from the wharfmen overhead to Ross. The wooden planks bowed slightly over her head with every step from above.

"Mrs. Wishart told me. She wrote them in a book."

"Well, I am glad for you about that, Ross. My mother wouldn't write any book. All she ever does is the work Miss Jane gives her. If she wasn't told what to do, she wouldn't know how to get out of bed in the morning." She resumed watching the men above. All she could see on most of them were their calves, but that was all right.

Ross's voice was slow. "I wish I knew what happened to her."

This time Gilly's whole body turned. "What? You mean you don't know?"

Ross shook her head, seeming surprised that Gilly had heard her. "No. I get the lessons, but that is all I know of her, what she wrote."

Gilly sat down close to Ross. Her face was a mixture of compassion and excitement. She took Ross' hand.

"Your mother's name was Angelica Laem. She was taken in by Mrs. Wishart when she was huge, and I mean huge with child, which was you. She was killed as a witch, for giving birth out of wedlock." She studied her friend's face carefully. Ross never betrayed much emotion, but Gilly knew her well enough to detect that this was having an impact. She waited.

"Angelica?" Ross repeated finally.

"Yes. But no one knows if this was her real name, or if she made it up to look like she was from a known country.

Because evidently she was really, really beautiful, and no one could place where she was from. She had sandy hair and black eyes, like yours."

Ross blinked self-consciously. She was quiet such a long time that Gilly was distracted and gazed back at the passing men. One foot paused, unmoving, over the floorboards of the bridge. They held their breaths. He backed up and kicked his toe in the crevice they looked out from, then his foot became a knee, and his hand steadied his lowering form toward their hideaway.

"Get out!" Gilly hissed. "Run now!" She and Ross sped like deer from their alcove.

⤚

The woods held Ross a long time before Gilly appeared in their meeting place beneath the firs. When the bobbing head of Gilly did appear, Ross knew something was wrong. Gilly made it up to the tree and stood outside of it, her hand held over her eye.

"What is it, Gilly?"

"Nothing." Ross stood and went to her. She was rubbing her eye with fury, her hair mussed from the press. Ross gingerly laid her hand on hers and drew it away for a closer look at the redness underneath. Gilly was crying.

"Is it a sting?" asked Ross.

Gilly shook her head. "Wood." She answered through tears.

Ross led her under the tree and set her down. "Stay here," she said. "And don't rub at it. I'll be back." With that, she was gone.

When she returned, Gilly was lying on her stomach, alternately blinking and rubbing at her swollen eye. Ross reached toward her with something on her fingers and brought them very close to her eye.

"Hey!" she cried. "What is that?"

"Ssh. It's flaxseed. Be still."

Gilly sniffed as her friend touched the substance onto her eye. She backed once and Ross caught her and leaned her forward again. Then she sat back and rubbed her hands on her skirt.

"Now leave it alone."

Gilly was staring at her with an interest that made her forget her pain. She lowered her hands and sat forward.

"Flax?" Gilly asked. Ross nodded. Gilly smiled. "So maybe I have an idea what you've been learning on Monday nights."

Ross glanced away, knowing all the while that it was useless under Gilly's scrutiny. She looked at Gilly sharply.

"So maybe I have an idea of what you've been doing on Monday nights as well."

Now it was Gilly's turn to look away. Her lips flapped open and shut, and she found her voice only after a complete forgetting of how it operated.

"What do you mean?"

"Oh, don't, Gilly." Her voice was cutting. "I am not stupid, and neither are you. We know where we stand."

Gilly was amazed. She'd never heard Ross speak like this, with such authority and brashness. She didn't know what to say. Ross stared away for a long time, and then looked at her, but Gilly had the impression that she was looking more at her eye than at her.

"That will draw out the splinter."

Gilly hiccupped.

"I'm sorry, Ross." There was another silence. Gilly couldn't take it. "I'm really sorry. I don't know why I did it. Maybe I just needed some excitement. I wasn't serious. I—I don't know what I was thinking. . ." She suddenly felt helpless.

Ross spoke calmly.

"It's all right. I know you. If I didn't, it might not be all right, but I understand you. So let it go."

A breeze carried around the tree, lifting leaves with a pleasant rush of sound. Gilly began to look herself again.

"So, you've talked to Johnathon?"

Ross smiled, half in response to the name, half at Gilly's predictability.

"More than once. More than you'd guess to know."

Gilly sat up on her knees. "When? How?"

Ross only smiled. Gilly felt thoroughly awake, and driven to inquire further, but her friend had forgiven her once, and she didn't want to push her again.

Miss Jane's men were a phenomenon. More of the old servants were dismissed or traded out of the staff as hulking workers streamed in from remote Scotch regions, highlands and valleys of the west. Her stiff skirts moved with straight lines as she led Alexander Thompson to the door.

"I'm telling you, you don't know what you're talking about. You should sell some of that land, and get back what you can now. Don't you see what a good amount of money I am offering you? And it's nothing but rocks!"

His face seemed to shift colors each time he spoke, the red vessels under his skin flexing and pulsing with each loud word he barked. Miss Jane remained placid as Rochie opened the door, her small dark eyes looking through him smoothly.

"No thank you, Mr. Thompson. The day I sell property will be the day Queen Mary builds a cathedral in Aberdeen. Good day."

He snorted, his thick eyelids quivering in his glare, and marched out. Rochie closed the door.

She turned just in time to face Gilly, who froze midstep in her tip-toe passing through the room. Miss Jane spoke with the same stoic authority that she had given Mr. Thompson.

"How's this? What duty have you to attend to in the house?"

Gilly still didn't move. Her voice was small.

"I was just ... passing through, Ma'am."

Miss Jane drew nearer her and examined her outright,

moving her head slowly over Gilly as one might a horse at market. Gilly pulled herself up and stood with her eyes staring straight ahead.

"Housegirl?"

"Yes, Ma'am." Where was her voice? "My mother is one of the nurses."

Miss Jane stood very close to Gilly's face now. Gilly felt her hands begin to flutter. Miss Jane's voice remained perfectly even.

"Her name is?"

Gilly blinked. For a moment, she honestly couldn't remember. Then the name exploded from her, at a ridiculously loud pitch, or so it seemed to Gilly.

"Jean."

"Full name?"

"Gilly Geillis Duncan." Her eyes closed in a fire of embarrassment. Miss Jane had surely meant the full name of her mother. Miss Jane, not as tall as Gilly, still stood looking directly into her face, her dark eyes so close that Gilly could see the thin hairs of her eyebrows from the corner of her vision. She tried not to look at her.

"What is it you do?"

Gilly's breath came a bit scant. "I do as my mother needs me to do." In her mind, she uttered a little prayer that Miss Jane would not follow up on this answer. But she didn't appear to have any measurable interest in Gilly. She dropped her gaze and walked toward the hall, Rochie right behind her. Gilly's whole body let go, her shoulders falling lower like weights, her head suddenly swimming over her loosened neck. She hurried out to the wood.

⁓

"Harrowing, just harrowing." Ross listened wide-eyed to Gilly's account. She herself had never been face-to-face with Miss Jane. "I thought she was going to slit my throat at any minute."

Strange how such a figure could have sprung from a woman like Mrs. Wishart, she thought.

"So where have you been all this time?"

Gilly's abrupt change of subject never caught Ross off guard, but the mere thought of Johnathon never failed to. Gilly smiled as the color rose in Ross' face, and she drew a little circle in the dirt with a stick.

"Well, I'm glad for you, Ross, I really am. If I had a man who looked like that . . ."

On and on her voice went, rising and falling in the usual cadence of her chatter about men and their bodies. Gilly was absolutely tireless on the subject. How good it must be for her, Ross thought, to be in the midst of Miss Jane's army. She was immensely glad that her friend had the surrounding to satisfy her fixation, but my goodness, she thought, what a bore. Ross looked at Gilly as she talked and thought of her encounter with Miss Jane. Plainly it had gone out of Gilly's mind completely, but perhaps it shouldn't have. The matter could prove more serious than she thought. Scarcely any of the original workers of the house remained from the new organization. If one could not prove oneself valuable to Miss Jane, and preferably this meant in brute physical strength, they were no longer here. A few specialized workers were still employed, in this job of nursing or spinning or such that men never seemed matched to.

"He's got these large hands," Gilly was saying. "Enormous. The backs are all hairy, but you can still see the lines of muscle moving as he grips things."

Maybe that was it, Ross thought. Maybe men were just too large and lumbering to perform fine work. Yet Johnathon performed a great deal of fine work, carving long, winding details through the legs of a table or chair, gouging in patterns, smoothing moldings with all the care a woman gives a bird fallen from its nest. But then Johnathon was not like other men. Not at all. Gilly's voice jabbed into her thoughts.

"To the wharf tonight!" She was chanting. "I say we hide out as long as we possibly can, and see what they do after dark. I bet they don't even work. they probably just sit on those wooden cargo boxes and swill ale and talk about women. There's a new one there who's Irish. You would faint to see his dark bushy eyebrows and ruff chin."

"Gilly," She stopped, startled at the sound of Ross' voice. She continued. "Gilly, do you want to stay here, working with the Wisharts?"

She looked surprised at the question. "Well yes, Ross, of course I do. Don't you? I'm sure you do. You have reasons to." She smiled at her again in that good-natured accusing manner. Ross didn't acknowledge this.

"Then you need a plan, same as Rena or anyone else. I'm all right, because of Mrs. Wishart. But you've been found out, and you're probably next on the list. I think maybe we should make you useful."

Gilly fell thoughtful. That won't last, Ross thought, and continued before the subject was lost. "You can't cook, can't sew; you aren't a giant, and, well, you just can't *do* anything."

Gilly began to look affronted.

"Now, I don't mean that as an insult. But you know what I mean. It won't wash with the new regime."

She nodded. "Yes, I know. I've thought of it before."

"Yes, anyone here would. But I'm thinking now that perhaps I can help you." Gilly looked at her. "Well, I have my specialized knowledge, and Mrs. Wishart said that if I didn't pass it on, it would be lost. That would make us the only two people to have my mother's secrets, and they are valuable. I think it's our only chance, Gilly."

Gilly felt her mood sober. Her friend was serious, and what she said was all true. She looked into her black eyes and heard herself speaking before she had thought it all out.

"All right, well yes, we should. If you want to, I mean." Ross shifted, the tangles of her hair catching the sunlight. Gilly was suddenly honored and hopeful. "Please, Ross. Would you? Would you teach me?"

Now it was Ross who smiled.

～

"I can't keep all of this in my head!" Gilly had a hand clapped over each ear, as if this would stop the stream of information. Ross was calm, as always.

"Of course you can. It's really not that hard. This herb—" she pointed to the wilting pile of green on the sun baked rock. "Is called Dragon's Wort. We dry it and crush the leaves to make a tea. We steep it in hot water until the water turns color, then drink it warm to calm the nerves, soothe a weak stomach or the pains of a young woman. Or we rub the root on aching teeth. The first time you know the pain of an aching tooth, you'll be grateful for this knowledge."

A shock of Gilly's pale hair fell over her eyes dramatically. "Ohh-" she moaned. "It's too much. Maybe I should learn to split wood instead.

"You'd have to know which trees to cut, and what the wood is like." Gilly flopped backward onto the ground. Ross continued, unfettered.

"This is one we had way back a month ago. What is it called?"

Gilly glanced over her shoulder and glowered at the bright yellow buttercups. "Frog's Foot." She said flatly. "To blister the skin in gout, and in tincture for scaling of the skin."

"Correct. Now sit up. We've got plenty more to do before the sun goes down."

Gilly's eyes brightened. "Well, some of us do, don't we? Speaking of wood . . ."

Ross held up a clutch of mustard seed. "Name?"

"Eye of Newt. Strengthens the memory, revives the spirits . . . expels heaviness, cures a crick in the neck."

"Very good."

Gilly sulked.

❧

"My dear, if that is what you want, you have my permission and my blessing."

Ross's eyes shined. Mrs. Wishart had that look of quiet joy, the glow of approval Ross had grown accustomed to and never failed to be cheered by.

"The wedding will have to be in the church, of course. I will do my utmost to attend, but if Mr. Wishart is not fairing any better, I am afraid I must only rely on your account. But I wish you happiness."

She nodded. "Thank you, Mrs. Wishart. It means a great deal to me to have your blessing. I daresay we hope to remain in service to the house."

"Of course," she said lightly. "Johnathon is a fine carpenter. He built the library with cleverness and taste. We consider him a fortunate asset to the Wishart house. You shall remain on as husband and wife. I will have a word with Miss Jane. I am sure that Jonathon's little shack could grow a bit onto its surrounding land."

"Thank you, Ma'am. You are so kind."

"Not at all. But now I have disheartening news for you." her blue eyes flickered a bit. "Your friend, Gilly, is being traded to an employer in North Berwick." A riot of color welled in Ross's face. Mrs. Wishart raised her petite white hand. "This is Jane's decision. I do not interfere with her decisions on running the staff, except that I have spoken as to your importance." Ross sighed without parting her lips. Mrs. Wishart continued. "She is being told this evening by Jane. She is to leave in the morning. I am sorry for you. I know she is your friend."

Ross was silent with turbulence. "Ross?" Mrs. Wishart leaned forward. Ross tried to smile but failed.

"I am sorry, Mrs. Wishart. Thank you for telling me. I

understand it is not your doing." She paused. "I am distressed."

Mrs. Wishart nodded sympathetically. "That is the end of our lesson tonight, child. Go to your friend. Tell her that perhaps you will visit her as a married lady. Go, child."

Ross rose. "Thank you, Ma'am."

The door closed behind her. Mrs. Wishart looked sadly after her, her eyes betraying much more emotion now that she was alone. She picked up the cane from behind her chair and began the walk back to her husband's bed.

～

"It's all right," Gilly said over-brightly. Her mouth was pulled tightly into a smile that did not reach her eyes. "Who knows? I might meet the man of my dreams there. Maybe this Mr. — , my new employer, will be promising. Who knows?"

Ross sat stiffly on the edge of her bed and looked at her. "Who is your employer?"

"David Seaton. He is the deputy-bailiff of Tranent."

"Where?"

"Just a small town. About ten miles from Edinburgh."

There was a silence. "Oh, well, you'll see Edinburgh."

"Yes, yes I suppose I will." The silence hung on. "I suppose I'll see Edinburgh."

Ross stood up and wandered a few feet, and with her back to Gilly, spoke.

"I am getting married."

She heard Gilly sit up without pushing down the blanket first. She was afraid to turn and see her face.

"To Johnathon? I mean, of course, you're getting married to Johnathon. Ross, that's, that's wonderful. It really is. That's really good for you." Ross finally turned.

"I'm sorry I didn't tell you before. I didn't mean to have this news on the same night that you got yours."

Gilly waved it away. She was practically bouncing in the flat bed. "No, no, that's all right; it's all right! I'm really happy for you!" Her eyes had the glint of her usual self. Ross sat back on the bed.

"But Gilly, I'm so sorry you're leaving. I mean, you're my only friend here, and we only just know each other, and I know how you wanted to stay."

Gilly's voice was high. "Well, you know how I like the wharf!" Her laugh caught too quickly and betrayed a sob. "I'll miss you, too, Ross. You know I will." She pushed at her eyes with the back of her hand. Her smile widened bravely. "But you'll come see me. I'll know it's you, when I see the finest crafted wagon in all of Scotland come rolling down my path, with a beautiful girl and a gorgeous man and all their children. We'll drink wine when you come!"

Ross clutched her suddenly, and they held fast in the night. Gilly pulled away. "Really, Ross, I appreciate your coming to see me. But I think I'd better get my rest before traveling so early in the morning. You understand." Her voice was light, but her eyes were full of water. Ross nodded and rose to leave. She looked as if she might say something, then thought better of it. Gilly called out a bit louder than needed be.

"Take care of yourself, "Miss Ross." And thanks for all the lessons!"

Their eyes met and they smiled, the moment lingering like a falling glass not yet reaching the ground. Then Ross turned and hurried out of the room. Gilly sunk down under the blanket.

⁓

The months wore on. Ross married simply, and Johnathon was granted freedom to work on their "house" in the back field. She continued her Monday evening lessons faithfully, filling her mind with all the lessons she could learn. Mrs. Wishart was proud, in her quiet manner, of how well she learned, and she herself never wavered in the teaching, despite the decline of her husband.

Then one evening, she handed Ross a package.

"Open it." Her eyes were pale twinkles. She looked tired, these days, Ross thought, and yet she never failed to find delight in things. She untied the knots in the strings and pulled away the brown paper. Good paper, strong paper, paper she could keep to sketch her plants and herbs onto. She was very careful about the corners. Inside was fine fabric, beautiful fabric, light and heavy, ruffles and tight-woven linen. She pulled apart the layers.

"Children clothes!" Her voice was a mere echo of her own. she held them up to the light. "They're beautiful." She put them in her lap and looked at Mrs. Wishart. "Too beautiful I couldn't possibly accept these."

Mrs. Wishart's eyes slanted with her warm glee. "They are rightfully yours, child. Those clothes were made by your own dear mother."

Ross cocked her head up. Her eyes were wide circles. "What?" She whispered.

"Yes, child. She made these for Jane, and when Jane outgrew them, they were put onto you, and then packed away for such a time as you might need them." She glanced candidly at Ross's stomach. "I think now may be such a time."

The color rose in Ross's face. "Thank you, Ma'am."

Mrs. Wishart patted her hand and started to rise. Ross rushed to hand her her cane and steady her.

"Thank you, child. I feel I must lie down now. But you go and show your husband what he must build a trunk to fit."

Ross guided her down the hall, her hands so young under those of Mrs. Wishart. She beamed with the vision of her babe in the fine garments she would be dreaming of tonight.

～

"Gilly has been accused of being a witch."

Ross sank down into a chair, her face devoid of life.

"The charge is that the Devil grants her powers to heal.

She cures "all such as are troubled or grieved with any kind of sickness of infirmity," said Mrs. Wishart. "She brews potions with herbs and plants, which are imbued with powers by the Devil, and in return, she allows him to suckle at night on her neck."

Ross's voice was but a whisper. "Go on."

"King James himself is presiding over the case, which is gaining fame as the case of the North Berwick witches. The King is being honored as a brave judge for approaching their purported power. He examined them at Holyrood Castle, and declared that these witches had flown over the sea to interfere with his boat. He insisted on knowing the names of the rest of her coven. Gilly was tortured until she agreed to the name of Agnes Sampson, a lady of some seventy years, educated and dignified. She was killed, very brutally. A schoolteacher of Saltpans was implicated as the coven leader. His name is Dr. John Fian. So far, one other woman has been killed in connection to the case, by the name of Euphemia Maclean. She was burned alive. A Barbra Napier is being tried now. Each is being wrenched for more names."

She stopped with the decisive edge that said that all of the known information had been let.

Ross stared ahead motionlessly. Mrs. Wishart watched her in silence. A long time passed. The lamps in the room dwindled their light to flickers that threatened darkness, but no one tended to their oil. No sounds came save the faint sounds of their breathing. Mrs. Wishart remained respectfully silent for such a time that she was sure at least an hour passed before Ross made a sound. When she did, it was an incoherent murmur, then another, then the sounds mingled and bent into fragile words.

"Will she be put to death?"

Mrs. Wishart looked at her carefully, surveying her black eyes and blanched pallor.

"Yes, my child. Gilly will be executed next week."

Ross delivered Siona in an atmosphere of fear and tragedy. As the exquisite infant came into the world, a wriggle of tiny pink limbs and large eyes, the lives of Gilly Geillis Duncan and Mr. Wishart were taken away, both victims of two very different plagues.

-5-

Asria's Road to Padua

They traveled in rapid and cloaked fashion through Scotland and England, stopping only far into the country, or in with rough-looking families Robert knew. Asria and Tommie tried to remain hidden, sitting in the back of the sturdy wagon, talking between themselves, and receiving the occasional gift from Robert of a new book. Robert did all the dealing with people there was to be done and brought her and Tommie food and drink.

Finally, what seemed an eternity later, they stopped in northern Italy. The travel had been exciting, but now Asria was elated to finally reach their destination. They settled into a modest house Robert's lovely wife had been holding, and both men seemed happier than she had ever known them to be. Asria herself was not interested in the domestic dailies of the house and the fanfare of reunion but disappeared from Robert and his wife and Tommie for afternoons and entire days as she had in the highlands, lost on exploration of this new and thrilling world.

Asria's head was constantly spinning. There was so much to see, and all so utterly new. What she wanted to see most of all was the University of Padua. *Padua.* She could say it plainly enough, and had an idea of which direction it lay. Robert had said that it was too soon, that she should simply become used to the new world first, and learn to properly dress herself, and move about the streets, use the shops and tools, and above all learn the language. He told her that what she spoke was in fact the oddity, instead of the language that these people spoke, and she should try to speak as little as possible, so not to draw attention to herself. He taught her in proper lessons, the rough transition from her obscure Gaelic dialect to vernacular Italian, and at the same time, mentioned English, Latin and Greek comparisons with enough frequency that she got it into mind that this was only the beginning. She was a quick learner, however, and it was not long before she was trying out her new tongue on street vendors and the odd passerby.

She was becoming accustomed to the way people and streets looked; she could use the logic of their way of life to make her way around the town and obtain what she needed. She read the street names and began little conversations with the men selling fish and wares. She ate warm and tanned breads, as Robert had promised, and a hundred different foods besides. She loved to eat. The buildings were straight and flat, not at all like the rounded, knobby stone cabins she'd always known. All around was a phantasmagoria of still newer and yet stranger things to see, to do, to taste, and to touch.

This day, the sun rose high and faded to a rosy pink on her skin as she walked. She loved seeing all the activity and the differences in people's faces. Most of the people here had black hair and light skin, though the men she saw outdoors often had their skin tanned from the sun like hers. As she walked farther, she eventually noticed the clothing of people becoming more elegant and somber somehow. The streets turned to brick, and it felt good under her feet.

Then she saw it. A library. A library in this small town, bearing the name of Medici. She picked up her bothersome skirts and ran full speed through people to the columns beneath the sign. She flew up the long, stone stairs, underneath the archway, and stopped dead center, gripping her arms, staring round and round the high ceilings, the regal walls. Her heart danced, and she laughed out loud. People stared at her. She was gone in a flash, with her bits of Italian and Latin, seeking out all the books she'd wanted to know.

Aeschylus, Aristophanes, Aristotle, Euripedes. Men. They were all men. Her finger quickly breezed over the names, leading her eye up and down the long rows of books. She stepped from row to row, lips solemn, brows knit in concentration. Dante, Virgil, Montaigne. Finally, her hand dropped to her side, and she walked up to the desk. She spoke loudly.

"Where are the women writers?"

His head jerked up from his reading. "Pardon me?"

"The women writers. These are all the men. Where do you keep the women's books?"

He shook his head as if he couldn't quite make out what she was saying. She wondered if her Italian was clear. She repeated the question in English, then carefully in Greek, which summoned about all the Greek she knew. His face contorted even more, the brows raising beyond incomprehension to complete astonishment and—what else? Horror? His twisted face made a laugh well up in her.

Suddenly an arm jerked her around. It was Robert, his face smoldering but contained. She was surprised more at the foreign expression than his spontaneous appearance at her side. He didn't look to her but said something quietly and formally to the man behind the desk. The man nodded in response and gave a little wave with the back of his hand. Robert took her arm decisively and led her out of the library, down the hard steps, and onto a wagon. They traveled for a long time in tense and utter silence, the sounds of the wheels and the city breaking the quiet pushing between them.

She knew what he'd said. He'd told the man that she was his daughter, and asked his pardon, and said that she was mad, but she didn't know the meaning of that word. She stared at her hands as his words kept repeating in her head, and the sight remained steady of Robert's angry face. But also remained the sight of the books, so many of them, thick volumes, most of the binders sewn by hand, name after name of the men who had written them. The thinkers. Well that there should be so many, but she wondered how long it would be until she would return to them, and browse through the books, study and learn enough languages to understand them, and read more, and find the other rooms, with more books, the books with the secrets of the caterpillars as Robert had told her and Tommie once upon a time in the cabin, secrets of the heavens, and the secrets that were told by the great men thinkers as well as the women.

Her thoughts were cut short by Robert's voice.

"You mustn't speak so in public, Asria. You especially must not use your Latin or Greek."

"But why, Robert?"

He leaned back that way that Papa did right before explaining something that he'd known for a long time.

"The world is not friendly with women scholars. It would have women at home, doing duties of the house and bearing and raising children. The way you trot about town now is unheard of for most women." He sighed. "I have raised you differently than the women you see about you. That is not your fault. What I have failed in is to teach you just how exceptional you are. You study, Asria. You read books. You speak languages of the learned man. This is not the way for women."

"Well, then, I can introduce something new to this world, which has shown me so much."

"No, Asria. What you also do not understand is the madness of the world today. In Scotland and in England, those people we saw hanging from gallows, do you remember?"

"Yes, I do."

"They were hanged because they were thought to be witches."

"Witches who traffic with the little people, Robert? I didn't think there were little people in that England."

His face was darkened with the weight of many thoughts. "No, child. This is not the kind of witchcraft you know of. It bears no relation to the faeries, nor to any of the little people. This witchcraft business, and those gallows, are the skeleton of the legal system today, the foundation of all religious superstition, and the blackest blight the world has ever known." He turned slightly to her. "This is what you must learn next, this horrible filth that you have not yet been sullied with. I had wanted to keep such ugliness away from you for as long as possible, but I see now that it can no longer be withheld. Such ignorance could be your undoing."

He looked at her carefully, looking at her sun-bleached hair, her intent black eyes, her ironically domestic garments he'd sewn for her himself, gathering the sleeves to allow for the hard, muscled arms underneath. She sat composed and waiting.

"This week we are going to court," he said. "You are going to witness a witch trial."

⁂

Robert dressed them in the stiff, pointed collars of the Puritans, and delivered them by the week's end to a small-town trial in northern Italy. Asria sat straight-backed beside Robert on a long, narrow bench where the spectators were gathering. No one exchanged greetings or engaged in conversation. The court opened with ceremony, and a woman was brought before the judge.

"The plaintiff Joseph Malarti accuses one Maria Vallenti of sending a blight on his crops. Plaintiff states Vallenti was seen to walk past his farm and spit on his soil. Since then, all vegetation has rotted, and the vines of the grapes have withered on their stakes."

The woman blinked very hard, almost beating her lids together when they met. The judge looked her over down to her feet and back up to her face.

"How do you plead?"

"I am innocent, your Honor. I never did such a thing."

"Are you in league with the Devil?"

She shook her head vigorously. "No, your Honor. I am a Christian woman."

"Is there further evidence?"

"No, you Honor."

"To the chamber."

Her blinks snapped her eyes more rapidly, and Asria noticed that she nearly lost her footing.

"Next."

"Plaintiff John Acuri accuses one Hattie Nelson. of sending a curse on his wife Riti, causing her to fall ill and rendering her sterile."

"How do you plead?"

"Not guilty, your Honor."

He looked at her closely.

"What is on your right cheek?"

She looked down.

"It is a mole, your Honor."

"This blemish is the mark of the Devil. This is prove of your marriage to him. When does he suckle you?"

Her hand went to her cheek. "No, your Honor. I never seen no Devil. Never. No."

The judge banged his gavel.

"The court judges Hatti Nelson to be a witch. Sentenced

to the confession chamber. If a confession is not had in one week's time, she will be put to death."

The woman cried out. Three men immediately restrained her, forcing her out.

One after another. Mostly women, though a few were men, and generally the children of the accused witch were brought before the bench. The women were plainly clothed, the sort one would pass at market or see coming down the church steps. The descriptions of the crimes all ran a common theme: the witch invisibly sent her spirit out to destroy crops, people, animals, bewitched pain and sterility on her victims, kissed the Devil's arse and offered herself to him in marriage. Yet the stories grew in color and proportion, becoming more fantastic with each case.

"Accused is said to have planted her spirit in a crow which laid its waste on the plaintiff's wagon. A mile later, a spoke in the wheel broke, and the defendant was sent sprawling into the road. The daughter of the accused was seen to have laughed."

One thing that did not escape Asria's notice was that out of all the cases, the hours upon hours of case after case being examined quickly so as to make time for more, not one single accused was found to be innocent. One woman was sentenced to hang for giving birth at the age of fifty-eight, a sure sign of tupping with the evil one. She watched the women as they were led to "the chamber," some crying, some trembling, others fixing the gravest of looks on their husbands as they were wrenched away. Some of the accused were cases already in progress, the witch not in question being brought for her inevitable and final sentence. These were the most horrible to see; most were bruised and recently scarred, and some could hardly walk for broken limbs jerking in uselessness; some had to be carried, and all were shaven completely bald. Teeth were missing, fingers and hands were missing, and so too was the glimmer of anything human in their eyes. Those were the tolerable sights. The most terrible Asria could not look at were those who did.

Robert and Asria left in silence as they had come, but much heavier. They boarded their carriage and set off south.

"That is how the world is right now, Asria," Robert said without precedent miles later. She looked to him as if glad to be drawn out of her own thoughts. "Germany is worse. Scotland is worse. And you know nothing of the torture. But you have seen all that is necessary. The world is indeed a dangerous place right now, and you must not take for granted your daily ability to leave our flat. All are at risk by virtue of being born, but 'tis a far graver danger to be born a woman."

"Those were women without significance," she checked herself. "I mean that, certainly they probably possessed some significance, but they were not extraordinary. There was nothing about them to attract notice."

He nodded. "Exactly. And you, and my wife, are women unique. You read, you write, your mind is trained, and quick, and tuned. You would be hard-pressed to find another woman, save royalty, who receives the education you do." He sighed. "And you are simply different." The carriage bumped along the dirt road. "You must be very careful, Asria. People should not know who you are."

She stared ahead into the horizon. "I am Asria," she answered. "I am named for the faery who passes unseen through the world of men."

The horses continued to clomp down the road.

⁓

The trunk sat across the room from her. She had never grown used to it. Most furniture, however strange or striking, eventually settles into background, receding from notice. One who sees a piece day after day for years on end finally takes it for granted, but not the trunk. On the contrary, its presence seemed to grow with every viewing, the old-fashioned but well-wrought locks and straps outlining a vitality and a life that forced itself into notice and dominated the simple room.

She stared at it. What was it that demanded such importance from inside that wooden box? She didn't believe its power was only relevant to herself, knowing it possessed a piece of her history. Its potency was keener than that; it was larger, and she knew that within its four small walls was a mystery that overshadowed them both. *I am Asria, and in my beginning, all that was was this trunk and me. I know what I am about. But this trunk is not as simple as I.*

It stood in the corner, regal with its stately lines and old wood, handsome, and something else. It belonged to her, but it was more than any human could ever claim.

A cold draft blew across the floor, ruffling her skirts slightly. She rose, breathing in the subtle smells of the trunk, of mystery and age. The house was quiet. She slipped out of her room into the sewing room. Out of the corner of her eye, she thought she caught the glimmer of a small spark lighting on the sill; she turned quickly, finding only the dark window. She felt around the tables until something stopped the flow of her hands, and lifted the silvery instrument in an enfolding grasp. She crept next into Tommie's room, pushing the door in softly and stealing inside beneath his heavy breaths. She gathered some items into her arms and crept back to her room.

She pulled back the curtains of the window. The pale light of the moon fell into her room, making a square of illumination on the floor. She knelt there, her long hair shining as if brushed with pixie dust. She inhaled deeply, letting the cool air of the night fill her lungs, and withdrew the sewing scissors. They laid cold and sharp in her palm. Her fingers drew through her hair, the sun-bleached tresses falling in webs over her shoulders before her. The breeze blew in a whirl round her kneeling form, lifting the waves of her hair. She raised a lock with her left hand, opening the scissors with her right. With the sharp, incisive sound that only shears possess, the lengths of her hair fell to the floor.

She pulled on Tommie's hose and fastened the waistcoat. She crossed to her bed with her gown, and laid it there to rest.

Before she left the house, she crept into Robert's room. His window was open, and through it a soft sound like the flutter of wings and tinkling laughter rose to her ears. She glanced sharply but saw nothing. Robert's breathing was low and long. His wife was a dark form beside him. She laid a note under his hand. The handwriting was exquisite.

Dear Father,
I have gone to Padua. Do not fear for me, for it is you who have taught me well. I shall always love you.
Your Son,
Asrian

It would be hours before the morning sun would rise on her new life.

～

"Padua? Well now, let's see, yeah, I can tell you. You walk up this road 'til you find a man who looks like me selling vegetables. That's my brother. He has great basil. Then you ask him which way to go, and you go on like that. That'll get you there."

She traveled for weeks, enough coins in her bag to see her stomach full for a while, enough novelty to see her mind full. She slept where she could, now and then being ushered out of warm doorways she had thought to be deserted, and here and again taken in by a kind soul sympathetic to a student. The conversations she heard helped her to learn things, how to buy a good piece of fruit, what sort of religious rage was going on where, the proper way to address a lady (and not to at all, to be completely proper), and also they taught her how old she was.

"Where you say you're walking?"

"Padua."

"A boy like you just going on to school? You had any schooling before? England? France?"

"No, sir."

The shoemaker grunted at her. "Well then, I suppose we'd better get you these holes patched up. You may be doing more walking than you think."

She settled here and there just to watch people, to look and listen and know. The days passed pleasantly, and she spoke with whomever she could. One late afternoon, a man of Tommie's age settled into conversation with her, and invited her for an evening ale.

"You really are brave, my friend, going into the university at your age."

"How old do you think I am?" She asked.

He considered her. "Well, I'd say between twenty and thirty. Cheer up. Maybe it'll give you a beard."

She laughed loudly and stroked her chin.

"Are you a student?"

He looked at his drink. "Was. Having a change of vocation now."

There was a note of wistfulness in his voice, perhaps even bitterment. She shrugged.

"Had a bit of trouble?"

He sighed. "Yeah, guess you could say." A silence fell between them. She waited politely.

"Sorry. I know I haven't been proper. Haven't introduced myself. Don't mean to be rude. Just that I'm so glad to find someone who didn't know my name."

She smiled. "No, I don't."

He looked across the room as if to insure privacy for what he was about to say. Then he leaned in.

"What do you know about witchcraft?" He asked in a low voice.

"Only that everyone's always talking of it, or thinking of it, or cringing about it."

He appeared pleased with her answer. "Have another ale, on me. I'll tell you some stories."

As the night wore on, Asria was riveted by the tales from her new friend, the young lawyer Marc Beardsley. He talked of the trials he'd seen, the iron wrath of the judges, the pale terror of women accused, and above all, the injustice. His manner of telling was straightforward and engaging. He asked what she wished to study. She looked startled at the change of focus, and glad to respond.

"Literature. Music. Science. Medicine."

"Medicine?" He asked. "That's witchcraft."

"Is it? It is based on process and logic, and the natural laws of things. It is science."

"We are manipulating these natural laws. That makes this witchcraft. Is not all of science witchcraft, particularly medicine? If things are left to go on without any sort of interference at all, we to merely study them, observe and record without any interaction or input at all, is that then the proper practice of things, anything beyond that constituting witchcraft?"

She looked hard into the space between them. "By definition, it must be witchcraft," she replied. "This is technical truth. But how much of the witchcraft business, and for that matter, the religious superstition on which is based, is founded on and organized by logic and technical truths? Myth is the imagination's logical answer for the unexplained and presumably unexplainable. Perhaps those who resist these phenomena being explained do so out of faith ingrained through long-time habit, or the wish to keep things romantic and settled for them. Myth, after all, eliminates the need for further research, or questioning, or the labors of adopting new ideas. Perhaps it is a faculty in the mind of the common man, a barrier that can only absorb information while young, for example, learning to speak one's native language, and once past a certain age, the capacity to induct new information rots and crumbles to nil."

Marc seemed gladdened by her response, but there were shadows in his eyes. "I think it is more simply the nature of people, Asria, the nature of people to want myth for all of its color as well as its answers. But I do agree that it is more the nature of the common folk. Today's scholars are trapped into this religious system, the domination of Knox, Calvin, the Church of England, the Puritans, and Italy's own Roman Catholicism. They must profess dogmatic belief in order to survive in society. But I would wager that if a study were made of the great thinkers over time, our time, from the Greeks, the Celts, and on forward for a millennium, that the true thinkers of science would on the majority rule out religion, even a belief in a god at all. That's what I'd wager. It is the business of science to explain rationally, as you say, and that in itself is the very antithesis of mythology."

They drank more ale in thought. She found his perspective fresh and unusual, and remarked so.

"Indeed, yes, it is so," he answered. His voice was heavy. "So unusual, in fact, my dear friend, that the world will not have it. My days are numbered, Asrian, because I have a curse."

She leaned even closer to him, tipping her ale and sloshing a bit onto the table.

"What is your curse, Marc?"

He put his face close to hers.

"I am cursed with the inability to bow before words I do not believe. My own thinking suffices for my creed, not any church nor philosopher nor king. Because of this, I am thought an ignorant man, and not worth listening to. But that is only part of my curse. The other part, the part which holds my doom, is this: no matter what the circumstance or the consequence, I must say what I believe to be right." He paused, the words holding weight between them in the night air. He lifted his mug to his lips. "Stay tomorrow, dear friend, and see how the world thinks. Tomorrow I damn myself. I had come out tonight to make my last toast to life."

With that, he raised his glass. Asrian did the same, not knowing what to do next. He tapped the bottom of her mug with the top of hers, raised it slightly, smiling. She did the same, smiling back politely with widened eyes.

~

The next day, Asrian watched the court proceedings, the morning and afternoon filled with the same gruesome spectacles she had witnessed further north with Robert. As the afternoon wore on, the wealthier of the accused were brought before the bench, and Marc spoke on behalf of those who had hired him. For the last half hour, he had been arguing a particularly fantastic accusation against his alleged witch with a sharp, clear voice. The woman was known to act as occasional midwife in the village, bringing blankets, prayers, and—the now questioned practice—cooking the bearing mothers thick soups to bolster their ravaged bodies. This was her witchcraft.

"But is all witchcraft evil?" He asked a clergyman.

"Of course it is evil. The Church states that all the witches must be killed. This is for those who cannot see the simple theological logic that anything manipulating the forces in this world or beyond other than God Himself is blasphemous and sinful."

Marc strode across the floor. "Do we ourselves not manipulate? I give to you that the grasping of a shovel, the breaking of earth with the shovel, the seed brought to such a place and dropped into the ground, the encouragement of such a plant to sprout and grow, and the taking of its harvest into the body are all in themselves and consummately amounting to manipulation."

"This is done by virtue of God, with his gifts the soil and the seed, under His all-seeing eyes, and strengthens us to carry out His will."

"And how is witchcraft wrought? By the powers of the

same nature, the earth, the water, the sun, the air. If God is to grant these, then it is our providence to use them. Under His eyes, you say. Yes, then, witchcraft is also under His eyes. The resulting strength is the same."

"These witches would send blight on their neighbor's crop, altering and stifling its growth as intended by its creator."

"Is your question, then, the question of intent, or simply whether it is permissible to use witchcraft at all, for any means?"

"Mine is not a question at all, sir. It is a statement that all witchcraft is forbidden, as it is in opposition to the power of God and all His Kingdom!" The clergyman's voice cracked on his last words.

"If these witches had not discouraged crop growth, but instead encouraged it, would this too be wrong?"

"All witchcraft is wrong. Anyone who knows the bible knows this."

"I call your attention to jurist Paulus Grillandus. In only 1525, not fifty years ago today, he marked history by not punishing beneficial sorcery, or white witchcraft."

"He didn't mark history; he marred it. Witchcraft is wrong, plain and simple." The clergyman said sulkily.

"What, then, is witchcraft?" Marc asked him.

"Witchcraft is manipulation by powers other than those of God, in fact, from the Devil."

Marc picked up a bound volume and held it before the court. "Would the court graciously indulge me this point? I have here a careful study conducted by Catholic theologian Joseph Artello. He wrote three impressive volumes on the subject of magic alone. His thesis is this: the types and methods of Magic are of infinite variation. He too defines witchcraft as manipulation, but leaves the source open-ended. For some, granted, it may be the Devil. But, he points out, that he has never discovered any witch acting in this vein who had not been taught belief in the Devil in the first place. In other words, in those lands yet to see a missionary, the Devil is not known to those people. They have no more an awareness of him than of God. So it is from religion to religion that no deity is recognized anywhere other than where its existence has been explained, and this includes the Christian god, God.

Some who practice witchcraft do so in their own name, some in the name of God, some in deities of which we do not know and have been taught (anyhow) to disavow, some simply in the name of the elements in nature, and some in no name at all. This last approach is of purely scientific ilk, without any glance in the direction of religion, nor relevance to."

"Heresy! Hear it! Hear it now!"

"If the name invoked be the issue, let the legal system fall into suit accordingly. As it stands now, the findings of these studies have not been recognized. The only possibility in the law as it stands now are that witchcraft is worked in the name of and by power of the Devil."

"Now he would attack the law! Bring him down! Who would defend the practice of a witchcraft but a witch himself!" The clergyman yelled.

"Might I also add that the Canon Episcopi condemned all belief in witchcraft as heretical and superstitious," Marc continued.

The judge spoke. "In 1486, the Malleus Maleficarum declared that belief in witchcraft is "so essentially a part of the Catholic faith that obstinately to maintain the opposite opinion savors of heresy. Your ilk have been drawing contradiction between the treatment of witchcraft through the Canon Episcopi, and the treatment of witchcraft through the Inquisition. But the Church has cleared this grey by stating that the witchcraft of the and the witchcraft of the Inquisition are different."

"Acknowledged. But, Your Honor, apparently there was a credo distinct and similar enough to warrant the Canon Episcopi at all, and I submit that this must be considered now, in the light of my argument. Granted that there was such credo, what faulty logic would destroy its probability for existence now? There are matters here so clear and logical that I am in the highest faith that the court is of such wisdom and sensibility as to recognize the need for exploration. We present our difficulties to the court, and the court is of such a nature that we may be confident that our concerns will be addressed. We must have our questions answered in order to proceed in the most unblemished conduct. In this spirit, we submit to the court: is the challenge to witchcraft one, its existence; two, the morality of its use at all; three, its origin and power; four, the user's intent; five, the results of its effects; or six, its true nature and definition?"

"Six points! Six points! A mark of the Devil!"

"We beg the court's inattention to pure superstition."

The judge raised his chin. "You may proceed, but be advised that the court regards you with a sternness and a firmness and has extended itself far beyond the call of patience. In addition, the court subscribes to the decrees of numerology. Proceed."

"Most humble thanks. This lawyer submits to the record that the defendant cannot be justly tried until these questions are sufficiently answered in the law. Further, no accused witch could be justly tried without these complications made clear. That is all."

"The court does not recognize these arguments. They question this court, the law, and the church. Witchcraft is easily defined and recognized. The court finds the accused witch guilty."

The woman screamed. He banged his gavel.

"Furthermore, the court orders a full investigation of Marc Beardsley, in the light of the heresies he has spoken here today." He banged his gavel. "Next."

Outside, the crowd was upheaval incarnate.

"Blasphemy! Pure hogwash blasphemy."

"Hang him. Hang him tomorrow before he sends a curse

on my crop and family."

Six men made their way unobtrusively to the roadside and murmured of murder. Had the village any room more for pandemonium, now it was complete. No storm could have caused a greater panic, no loosed criminal a larger alarm. Doors were bolted quickly though the dim of eventide had not yet begun. No neighbor dared speak or be seen by another. Again and still, the danger of living outweighed anything they had ever known.

Asrian hoisted her trunk onto her back and walked quickly on. She knew she would never see her young friend again. She traveled more rapidly after that, sometimes hiring a carriage to take her south faster. She knew she needed the world which loved books, and hoped fervently it would still exist when she got there.

Her travels went more quickly, as she moved south, the villages turning to towns, the towns growing more colorful and metropolitan. She wandered into the art galleries, smooth walls hung with the beautiful pictures that were windows to still more worlds, magical pictures that surely contained life itself. She loved the sharp, definite faces of Botticelli, and the softer forms like Van der Weyden. She was particularly fascinated by the surrealists, took herself out of her way to view work of Hieronymus Bosch, the Dutch painter, and his 'Vision of Tondalys.' She gazed without a word for hours at the weird figures, a strange animal working a stick through a free-standing colossal ear; another indefinable being stretching its mouth wide, revealing inside it many people gathered round a table; people flying through the air; a giant hat trapping a man whose leg is growing roots; the fire blazing in the sky. Her mind tried to absorb it all, and, if not make sense of it, then at least know it, keep the image etched in her mind for periodic withdrawal and reexamination. These things seemed to be the subterfuge of the world before her, the silhouettes of this bizarre world. Perhaps the little people saw things this way.

She wandered far away into the finer churches, and stood still right in the middle of the aisles, craning her neck to see the figures that seemed to lift straight away from the ceiling, at other times sink far into it, away from her and anything on the ground which might reach them. They were real, they were life, these figures, and she collected them in her mind to recreate later in her dreams at night.

She loved the gardens, the paths flanked with myrtle and rosemary, the statues and grottoes becoming covered in winding vines and ivy, the maidenhair ferns girding the miracles of fountains. Of course, there were the flowerbeds, full of hyacinths, lilies, jasmine, roses and gillyflowers. She beamed at these until her cheeks grew ruddy with joy, and hurried on for the next delight.

And then her dream was realized. Suddenly she found herself one day seated at a lecture, a student like any other in the great University of Padua.

They taught her first ancient history and philosophy, relishing the Greeks and Romans as humans who had maximized their potential. She attended lecture after lecture, riveted utterly by the amount of knowledge the teachers held in their minds. A flash of thrill sent wetness to her eyes as she put out her hands and embraced her first text: the Latin grammar of Donatus. Hours upon hours she devoted to painstaking conjugation and memorization of the classics, reading the Latin of Cicero, rising before the sun to consume one more poem of Virgil before the University whirred into life.

In the area of medicine, Padua boasted a revolution in the teaching approach. Breaking with tradition, the teachers in its anatomy theater dissected cadavers themselves to demonstrate during lectures. Previously, the man of learning, who gained knowledge by reading, was keenly distinguished from the manual laborer, the barber-surgeon, who actually cut up the body.

She loved it. She was in Padua. She was home.

- 6 -

The Aberdeen Witches: Siona's Curse and the Downfall of Janet Wishart

"Mother is to have a personal girl with her round the clock, to do her bidding and nothing else. The girl will be kept just as privy as the nurse to Mother's every health detail, and it is the duty of both to make Mother as completely comfortable as possible. This includes indulging her whims, albeit respectful to the doctor's orders."

The nurse nodded, feeling slighted in Miss Jane's presence. "Yes, mum."

"I am putting the girl on task beginning tomorrow morning. You may know of her. Her name is Siona. She lives in the back cabin. She is thirteen years old, and quite capable. She is quiet and obedient. You will work well together."

The nurse nodded again, thinking Miss Jane must mean the young daughter of the carpenter and his wife who lived behind the house, the only child who remained on the Wishart grounds. She had seen the girl moving about more than once, a shyish girl with the beginnings of a woman's body. Not that she was given to thoughts on such things, but it was a striking thing, the first thing that impressed anyone who saw her. Siona had more of a more of a woman's body now than most women ever do.

Miss Jane drew herself up. "I will bring her on tomorrow morning. That is all. Good night." She left.

The next morning found Mrs. Wishart extremely delicate, fading pale on the sheet. The nurse tended to her water as Jane stood beside the bed a tender girl whose plain clothes could not hide her ripening sensuality. Siona was a blossom, with glossy light auburn hair and light pink skin. Her eyes trailed up the towering four posters and fixed wonderingly on the canopy. Mrs. Wishart watched all her with evident pleasure, her eyes moving with Siona's to know each next novelty that engaged the girl's eye.

"This is Siona. Siona will be with you all of the time. She knows her way around the place and may move freely through the main house. Use her as you like."

A trifle unsuccessfully, Mrs. Wishart pulled herself higher on the pillow. She caught her breath and smiled kindly at the girl. Siona faced the woman, looking carefully into her face, and shyly smiling at the pale blue eyes. The lines in Mrs. Wishart's face outlined some secret message to the girl, and Siona's face smoothed with understanding. Jane satisfied herself that everything was in order, and kissed her mother on the forehead.

"I leave you to a new day. I must go into town and will see you sometime in the evening. Be well. Good day, Siona."

"Good day, ma'am."

"Goodbye, Jane. Enjoy the town."

Her brisk steps disappeared into the hall, followed by the heavier steps of Rochie, and the nurse laid out fresh clean linens. Mrs. Wishart's eyes were on Siona.

"How do you do, Siona?"

"Fine, thank you, Ma'am." Her voice was small.

"I knew your grandmother and I know your mother. Your line boasts beauty and sharp, active minds. The Laem women like to think. What do you think of, in your young mind?"

Siona stepped closer. She liked the tone in this woman's voice, and was fascinated with her age. She had never seen such an old person. Her bluish hands trailed out on the blankets, her nails ridged and yellow. The woman saw her stare and laughed.

"You may ask me questions about being old, Siona. I will tell you anything you like."

Siona smiled fully. Mrs. Wishart was like nothing she had ever known.

❦

She knocked on the door. Silence. She knocked again. This time the door opened, revealing a giant of a man. His rough working clothes showed the wideness of his chest, and the thickness of his arms. He stared at her.

"Miss Wishart sent me. I am the housegirl."

He seemed to examine her, judge something passing, and reluctantly opened the door. "All right. Set those things over there."

She looked to where he was pointing. The whole of the inside was taken up with black equipment, hanging iron claws, tongs, poles, hammers, crooks. A black forge towered on the far side of the room, made even starker by the presence of a huge bellows. A worn work table reached along the side wall, its corners rounded through use. She stepped in hesitantly. He was busy at something on the other side of the room, his broad back to her. She walked carefully over to the table and set the sack on top of it. The table was mostly clear. The tools were so foreign, so malignant seeming, with all of their points and angles. The room was dominated by his heavy dark anvil, looming up in the center of the room like some menacing creature protruding from the sea. The room was hot, to, as if a southern summer stagnated inside. If there were any windows, they were covered enough by the clutter that she couldn't see them.

"What'd you bring?"

She jumped. He was right behind her. She tried to answer and realized she'd completely forgotten.

"Um . . . some oats, and some fish, and two loaves of bread."

He grunted and reached into the sack, withdrawing a loaf and setting it firmly before her. "Eat some."

"Oh, no thank you. I am not hungry."

He snatched the bread off the table, unwrapped it from its towels, and cut it suddenly with the smack of an iron knife. It lay before her, white inside.

"Eat some." He turned and walked back to the table he'd been working at.

She took the hunk and chewed it, feeling the dryness of her mouth. There was an odd smell to this place, the smell of molten metal and something burnt. She moved a little toward the tall forge, fascinated, and peered inside.

"Melt iron there. Gets very hot."

The bread caught in her throat. He'd come up behind her again.

"Thank you for the bread. I should be getting back now." She was halfway home before she realized that the remainder of her piece of bread was still in her hand.

The next day, Siona was relieved to find her way into the far bedroom with its luxurious curtains. Everything about Mrs. Wishart was a trifle overdone, a ruffle here where purely superfluous, and she reveled in the lovely eccentric frivolity of it all. She held Mrs. Wishart's silverware for her as she ate, on the days when she couldn't quite manage it herself. It was real silver, not like the thick wooden spoons that her father made for them to use in the cabin. The mornings lasted forever in that far bedroom with the long windows her father had put in himself, the light growing and washing everything as white as Mrs. Wishart's long, ancient hair.

Her mother had seemed gladdened by Siona's new duty, and this encouraged Siona even more to feel secure in enjoying it. Whenever her mother mentioned Mrs. Wishart or the other way around, a spark came to her eyes, a spark of confidential fondness that they each matched in their separate places of living. It was all wondrous to Siona, and mysterious, and she saddened at the thought of leaving her fragile and happy mistress. But it happened whenever Miss Jane or one of the nurses had an errand for her to run. With luck, these avulsions led her only to another section of the house, and once finished, she could quickly return to the tall postered bed. But once every week, Miss Jane sought her out with a brown package to be taken to Mr. Webster. Siona didn't like the aversion that surged through her with every mention of the blacksmith, thinking it unwholesome and an unpleasant aspect of her that reared its ugly head in the midst of all this misty pleasure and sought to allay her feelings. But as Miss Jane's stiff footsteps carried down the hall, Siona felt the bad thoughts well up in her again.

"You will take this package to Mr. Webster," Miss Jane had said, and Siona had dutifully bid farewell to Mrs. Wishart and left the house.

The sky was grey. She didn't want to go back to the blacksmith's house. The dread of it preceded her every step, the smell of something smoldering, the dark heavy tools, the strange man. The dirt road stretched long before her, seeming longer than it ever had. Her steps were sluggish, and she knew she shouldn't walk too slowly. The sun was already high behind the clouds. The air was a bit chilly, and would be moreso on her walk back.

Again she had to knock twice before he answered. He was dressed just the same. He must always where nearly the same clothes for his work, she thought vaguely. His leather apron was almost the same dun as his skin, or was it the other way around?

He stared down at her. She held the package out with both arms.

"There's fish here," she stammered, "and some rawhide Miss Wishart said you need."

"Set it over there." She moved to escape his eyes and put the sack on the table. There were metal objects lying about, odd unfinished shapes, and massive swage blocks standing with all the weightiness of headstones. She turned to leave.

"Good day."

"Come here." He said. She stood still from pure surprise. "Hold this."

He loomed close to her, holding out an iron rod a little wider than she. He was dirty, the kind of dirtiness that seemed so sunk into the skin that it would never scrub clean, ringing his knuckles and pushing out from under his fingernails. His skin was shiny, from oil or sweat, and she could see scratches and burn marks all over his arms. Her throat felt too narrow to breathe through. He grunted.

She took the rod with both hands, dipping slightly with the weight.

"Stand there."

She moved backwards, picking up her feet slowly, trying to peer behind her to find whether the path was clear. His arms hung at his sides. A dig into her middle back told her she was as far against the wall as she could reach. The forge rumbled low beside her, and its heat made the surfaces of her skin nearest it suddenly grow hot. She looked at him. He sat at the main table across from her, withdrawing bread from the sack and placing it before him. He unwrapped it, taking care to lift each corner of the towel and lay it out on the table before beginning the next.

The muscles in her arms pulled taut under the growing weight of the rod. She felt an ache on the insides of her elbows, and tried to stiffen her wrists. He lifted the bread from the open towel and put the towel back into the sack. His hands were making black prints on the loaf. He had large hands, so large that one could span the height of the loaf, and his fingers wrapped round it like claws.

The heat was rising in her face now, pressing and making her blink. A thin trickle wove its way from the hair over her temple, running down close to her ear and leaving at her jaw. The next trickle followed its path but kept tickling along the line of her jaw, gathering under her chin and dangling there as if it would never leave. Her arms ached.

His eyes never left her. He tore off a piece of the bread, raised it, and pushed it into his mouth. Her arms trembled under the weight of the rod. It was growing hot with her skin, only more quickly. She swallowed. He chewed slowly, his stare boring into her. His face was shiny with grease, streaked where his fingers had wiped through. She tried to look past his eyes to the doorway. He took another bite, his jaw moving up and down under the steady fix of his stare. Her throat constricted, her breathing coming faster. Her back tightened and ached, shoulders pulling in to support the rod that was sinking below her belly. Sweat ran into her eyes and stung. Her arms shook violently, the skin feeling on fire. Her backed arched as her body lowered, she trying to jut out her arms, but they disobeying, the rod pushing deeper into her. Her legs flexed once and jerked out of her control, the shock of it reverberating through her body, jolting her arms. They fell and the rod slammed onto the ground, barely missing her toes. She lurched forward and her legs scrambled to keep her from falling. Her arms hung dead. He tore off another piece of the bread.

Her whole body trembled, and her heart raced so fast it hurt. She looked at his eyes which were still staring at her, forced herself upright, and ran across the room as quickly as she could. Her hand fell on the door and she fumbled with the lock, fingers too strained to move properly. Finally it gave and she pushed open the door, fleeing into the road. He took another bite of the bread.

She lay awake, staring into the darkness. She wanted a bath. Miss Jane had given her more chores to do when she'd gotten back, and she had done them all, including cleaning fish out behind the house. Tiredness overtook her and she'd blown out the candle, but now that its light was gone, she found herself completely awake, but immensely weary. Beneath her loft, her mother and father slept soundly, the sound of their breathing good to her. She rubbed her hands together. The night seemed to go on forever. She wished the morning would hurry and bring her the sunlit windows of Mrs. Wishart. She sighed. Next week, she would have to take Mr. Webster his next package.

When she went to Mrs. Wishart's door, Miss Jane stopped her and led her back into the house. Siona was weak, and nearly lost her balance as she followed her down the hall. Miss Jane stood before her in the dining room. Siona had the stray thought that she had never seen Miss Jane sit down.

"Siona, you have served my mother well. She has been glad for your company."

Siona couldn't hear the words exactly right. She knew it was something she wouldn't want to hear. Miss Jane kept on.

"Mrs. Wishart is doing poorly. It would not be a good idea for you to pester her now. You will help with the cleaning of the main house, and do scrap work for Lindsay as need be. But unless I tell you differently, do not go into Mrs. Wishart's room."

Siona felt numb. Not just a numbness of the limbs, and the fingers, but numb in her sight, and her hearing, with the distinct sensation that if she spoke, no sound would come. She didn't feel capable of forming a thought. Miss Jane set her in the kitchen to work under Lindsay. Lindsay was Rena's daughter. Rena had passed away long before Siona had been here. Squat Lindsay and her coarse manner set Siona about to little tasks the day long. Siona stared at the vegetables as if they were foreign objects and wondered blankly at the obedience that her body gave to orders. She watched it was if from a separate corner of the room, and tried to look away when Miss Jane walked in with the brown package and handed it to Siona. Her arms took it, and much as she hoped her legs wouldn't do it, they began to walk to the blacksmith's place.

≈

She knocked. When no one answered, she bent down, quickly set the sack before the door and made to leave. Before she had risen, the door opened, and there was the soiled face of Mr. Webster. She stepped backwards, looking at him, and in a flash of thought, turned to leave. She felt a clamp on her wrist and the sack swung out of the doorway. She was inside and the door was being bolted. He led her to the anvil, the furnace glowing orange in the dark interior. He had no lamps burning. He pushed her wrist down and she bent under the pressure, her skirts meeting the dirt floor. He took both her wrists in the same hand and a rope in the other, and wrapped them together. He coiled the rope around the leg of the anvil, drawing her hands against its warm metal and knotting the rope several times on the other side. Her heart felt too large for her chest, and she winced under the pain of its hard, rapid beating. She looked up at the iron throat, its curve the reaching neck of a lizard. Already the sweat was breaking from her hairline and her hands, which were soiled from his blackened palms. The furnace surged and he pulled off his shirt, revealing a chiseled and expansive chest. Siona had the vague thought that he must wear his apron. He took a pair of tongs from the wall and went to the furnace. He opened its door, the room flooding with yellow light and a blast of heat. He inserted his tongs and drew out a long narrow piece of iron, glowing more unnaturally than anything she'd ever seen. She blinked to clear the wet from her brow and her eyes. The thing was too bright to look at.

He sat at the anvil, his boot on the trail of her skirt, and cracked a splitting smack into the smoldering silence with his hammer. Then came another, and another, she hiding her head in her shoulder and bosom to avoid the falling sparks. His smacks were powered and systematic, mounting in speed and intensity. She rubbed her eyes into her shirt to mop her tears. Her hair laid hot against her face. His hammering grew in volume, a relentless pounding that sent a shock through her with every blow.

⟡

Her mouth was slack. She tried to make her hand lift, but could not summon the will. Miss Jane had needed her to deliver two packages, instead of the usual one. All day she had not even seen Mrs. Wishart. The day had blessedly ended and Siona lay in her bed. In the light of the candle, she could see the bruises leading up between her legs. She shifted slightly, and winced, the burns breaking open again. She tried hard to stop the evil thoughts, the horrible flashes of the room, and his wretched skin, and just as awful, the evil thoughts she herself was having. She didn't like Mr. Webster. She knew Miss Jane must, but she didn't, and she didn't think that he was a good man. In fact, she thought he was a bad man, an evil man, who did bad things, and as her breath sucked in to keep her fever of hatred unknown to her parents below, she wished, in her deepest of misery, that he would die. Yes, as her brain swelled inside her skull, she wished he would die, and be forever gone, and never touch anyone again. The tears ran hot on her cheek. If she reached down there again, the new pus would be sticky.

⬱

Four men burst into the house. Siona's head had snapped up from her scrubbing, and Miss Jane had rushed into the room, thrown aside by the looming Rochie for protection.

"What is the meaning of this?" She demanded; she did not shout.

Without a word, one of the men swung a large leather sling with a large rock in it against the temple of Rochie. He went down immediately. Siona screamed. The tallest of the men, whom Siona recognized as a man of the law, stepped forward and unrolled a paper.

"We have a warrant for the arrest of Miss Janet Wishart, Ma'am. You are ordered to appear in court tomorrow morning. The court will detain you until then."

Her eyes flared.

"On what and whose charge?"

"'Tis a charge of witchery, Miss Wishart. The witching of a Mr. Alexander Thompson, and of a Mr. Andrew Webster. You will be coming with us."

Miss Wishart cursed. The men instantly swarmed around her and wrenched her arms behind her back. One gave her three sharp blows to the face, and she cried out. The man with the warrant replaced it in his bag and nodded his head toward the door. They twisted her toward it, her neck bent from the ferociousness of the blows. Though she did not resist, the men shoved her roughly out of the house, and left the door open. In a flash, six men entered the house and dispersed in every direction, some going upstairs, some down the hall, one toward the kitchen. The man in the receiving room with Siona immediately moved to the chest against the far wall, yanking its doors open and overturning it despite its weight, spilling its contents onto the floor. He rifled through them, spreading them out as if looking for something, and then tapped and punched at its bottom in search of another compartment. Siona huddled into the corner, her knees drawn up against her chest, watching the men collect various things and destroy others, looking even between the plates in the plate cupboard, and under the rugs on the floor. A man who had been stomping from room to room shot down the hallway, and she heard his steps lead into the library.

"Eureka!" He hollered. The other men thundered to see what he'd found.

⁕

"They ain't no chance for us," said Lindsay. She shook her head, standing as if lost in the ruin of her kitchen. All of the pots and pans had been strewn about, the oven and cupboards rooted through, and all of the food torn and upset. Several of the servants had gathered here and sat around the room in various attitudes of despair. Lindsay's voice was heavy and low.

"Ole Miss Wishart's done. We may's well run south, with the speed of God."

Siona crouched in an open cupboard.

"But what's she done?"

Lindsay looked down at her.

"Nothing, child. She ain't done nothing. But that don't matter."

There was a silence. One of the men from the wharf spoke.

"Thompson dead. Webster dead. Don't know about that, Lindsay."

Lindsay turned on him with spontaneous fury.

"Miss Jane may not be the friendliest, but she ain't done us no wrong. We got enough to eat, now, don't we?"

"We fish it out!" another cried.

"And I fix it," she retorted with a sneer. He looked at the ceiling.

"You know what this means," a short man who had been sitting quietly on the table spoke while rubbing his nose. "Means them western Wisharts going to be breathing down our necks sun-up to sun-down. They just been waiting to pick up the reins."

Lindsay sighed.

They picked through some of the refuse enough to put together something to eat, and found some ale left in the casks. Siona was staring at Lindsay.

"Gotta eat, child. No time to be taking sick now."

Siona's voice came very small.

"What do you mean, Mr. Webster?"

Lindsay patted her hand. "He's dead, child. The forge spat the wrong way, he got it, and he's dead. Court says it's Miss Jane, witched him."

Siona's arm gripped around her own middle.

"You ill?" Lindsay set down her food. The girl had fallen completely white, and apparently couldn't speak.

"See here, now, you eat something. Miss Jane ain't killed nobody."

Two of the men guffawed. Lindsay hissed at them and threw spoon at one. "Behave yourselves."

The men chided one another and poured more ale. Siona crawled deeper into the cupboard.

❧

Siona was hauled onto the wagon with the other servants of the house. Her parents weren't with her. The road underneath was dodgy, and the long ride to the courthouse was rough. They rode in silence, and when it stopped, they all got off in movements without hurry. She was lifted down and set onto the ground.

The courthouse was full of people. They stared, the same silence seeming to be brought inside the high flat walls and set over people like bricks. She followed in the line of servants to their seats on the long benches and didn't notice her leg being pushed against that of the servant next to her. She still couldn't think.

People were all around her, people she knew, people she'd seen, people she didn't know. She saw them, standing in their long robes, their mouths opening and shutting like fish, people rising, sitting, going forward or walking away as the speakers commanded. What was it that was so dark, what was it that was so impossible about all of this? Oh yes, it was Miss Jane. There she was, her small but straight frame, her dark eyes clouded by a bruise. The judge was talking to her, his mouth moving up and down. Men were nodding, they were staring at Miss Jane, they kept their mouths straight lines and didn't move their eyes. Miss Jane was standing before the judge, her hands tied before her. The words were a drone. She couldn't separate the syllables. Then they started to emerge from the blur.

"Mr. Thompson was more than once seen to leave your company in considerable disconcertion. You made a remark involving the Church, did you not?"

"I said to Mr. Thompson that the day I sold property would be the day Queen Mary built a cathedral in Aberdeen."

There was a murmur that swallowed up the next sentences. Men made sharp remarks, some leaning forward, some growing red in the face. Siona couldn't feel her hands. Time seemed to drag on for an eternity, Miss Jane standing there frozen, the men making waves and waves of low sound. Someone moved against her leg and the words came clear again.

"Mr. Andrew Webster was the honored blacksmith of Aberdeen and surrounding villages for years. He was a reliable man skilled in his craft. Is it not true that you, Miss Wishart, were responsible for much of the food he ate?"

Miss Jane spoke tersely. "I sent him groceries weekly."

"Why was this, Miss Wishart?"

"Mr. Webster was held in esteem by previous generations. The tradition of sending him food in exchange for the services he rendered us had been established long before me."

"By whom, Miss Wishart?"

Miss Jane was silent. Something was even more wrong.

"I asked you a question, Miss Wishart. The tradition of sending Mr. Webster food was established by whom?"

Miss Jane had hatred in her eye. "My mother." She flung the words like spit at the judge. There was movement in the back of the courtroom, people moving aside and making way. Then Siona watched as Mrs. Wishart herself was brought before the judge, and made to stand beside Jane. Siona's heart jumped. This was the first she had seen of Mrs. Wishart in a long time. Men had to support her; she could no longer stand on her own. And Siona could see some of her profile. Her skin was even more pulled along her bones, her cheekbones covered by the film of cobweb that was her skin. She wanted to see her eyes. Just let me see her eyes, she thought. Just once, that will be enough. Just let me see her eyes.

"Mrs. Wishart, your daughter Janet declares that it was you who began the tradition of sending Mr. Andrew Webster food. Is that right?"

Her head shook several times before her voice came. When it did come, it was so faint, the judge had to lean forward to hear. Siona's eyes misted at the edges of her faint words.

"You say that you did. And did you, perhaps, have any malice toward Mr. Webster?"

She shook her head more vehemently, using the rhythm of the jerks that already moved her head and neck from side to side. The judge put his chin up.

"The court finds that, as Mrs. Wishart saw to the groceries for years preceding Miss Janet Wishart, and as Mr. Webster suffered no malady therewith, the question of witchery lies only on the shoulders of Miss Janet Wishart. Mrs.Wishart may sit for the time being."

There was that stream of murmuring again, released like a jet in a leaking pipe. Mrs. Wishart was led back down to her bench. She stumbled on the way, and Siona rose slightly out of her seat. The men grabbed her up, and she hobbled along again. Siona lowered herself tensely. Just look up, Mrs. Wishart, please, just let me see your eyes. But she was gone.

"Is it not true that you owned the land Mr. Webster's cabin stands on?"

"Yes." Miss Jane spoke the same as she always had, no matter her mother had just been beside her, no matter her house had been turned out, no matter that she was on trial for her very life right now. Siona's eyes moved to the front of the judge's wooden stand. The men were talking of Miss Jane, that she had never taken a husband, that she ran the Wishart house with her peculiar army of men, that the profits of the Wishart wharf had increased drastically since she had been operating things. There were more problems. She could read. She could write. There were books in her house. She signed papers and contracts. She figured money. In sum, Miss Jane was an unnatural phenomenon. Miss Jane was in league with the Devil.

"When did you sign your soul to the black man?"

"I have never sworn anything to Satan."

"When did you first see him?"

"I have never seen Satan."

"Where does he suckle you at night?"

"I am not suckled by anything."

Siona heard all the words now. They were coming out of the speakers more rapidly. It was all accelerated, the questions shooting from the judge in rapid-fire. Siona heard the tops of their consonants. She heard their breathing, and the breathing of the person next to her, and the breathing of the person in the last row. She heard the scratching of an insect on the windowsill.

"What were your first orders?"

"I have had no orders from Satan."

"Who else have you killed?"

"I have not killed anyone."

"Give us all the names of those whom you have killed."

"I have not killed anyone."

Siona's heart was too large for her chest. Her eyes were too large for their sockets. She heard the roar of blood in her head, and felt her blood vessels squeezing under her skin, pushing out her limbs, her neck, and her face. She was on fire.

"How did you kill Mr. Andrew Webster?"

"I did not kill Mr. Andrew Webster."

"How did you kill Mr. Andrew Webster?"

"I did not kill Mr. Andrew Webster."

"How did you kill Mr. Andrew Webster?"

"I did not kill Mr. Andrew Webster."

An explosion ripped through Siona. She shot out of her seat, standing in the middle of the aisle, completely blinded by the flames before her eyes. Her voice tore her throat raw.

"I killed Mr. Webster! I killed Mr. Webster! Not Miss Jane! She didn't kill anybody! I killed Mr. Webster!"

Six men leapt and held her like a vise. All eyes were on her. The judge spoke low.

"How, child, did you kill this man?"

Her very body was scalding to her. Her head swayed back and forth until a large hand held it in place. She caught some breath. Her voice was very quiet.

"I lay in bed, and I wished him dead." She said simply.

The judge sat back. He stared at Siona. The courtroom was without a sound. The deputies and the bailiffs and the attendants all fastened their eyes on the judge. His focus was steady on the full young girl before him. Her eyes were wild. Her face was so deep red it was nearly purple. He spoke in a very calm and orderly tone.

"The court finds Miss Jane Wishart guilty of the murder of Mr. Andrew Webster, by method of bewitching this child, and sending through her innocence, her own black curse. Take the girl to the confession chamber. She will be tried as a witch at the next court opening. Resume the trial." He banged his gavel once.

Siona's eyes rolled to the back of her head. The men turned her, holding her limp body by the angles of her shoulders and elbows. Her head fell back, her mouth open and jarring with each step they took. The rear bailiff opened the courtroom door. Her head fell to one side, her swollen face tilting toward the pale figure in the back row. Siona's eyes, wide open, black and glassy, met the eyes of Mrs. Wishart. But they were closed.

-7-

Asria and William Harvey: The Witching Hour

Asrian walked down the familiar hall. The clip of her heels and her long legs carried her quickly through crowds, and she often made a game of memorizing the backs of heads as she passed them, and keeping tally: one blonde, two brunette, black hair, white hair, brown, brown, black. The stretch pulled pleasantly in her thighs as she breezed past person after person, with hair of varying lengths. But one head was remaining in front of her despite her long strides. She concentrated on this brown hair falling slightly below the shoulders and increased her pace. She neared him, but he held a quick gait. She passed more, black hair, black hair, brown, light brown, almond, and finally drew up not five paces behind the competitor. He turned his head slightly and she could see part of the profile of his face. He was obviously English, young, with pale skin. She pushed forward on her toes. He was veering to the right, moving through the crowd toward the wall. She followed his path. His gait was slowing a little, and becoming irregular; his body tipped a bit to the side. He nearly lost his balance. He reached for the wall. She sprung toward him and reached him just in time to catch his falling form in her arms. She lowered him to the floor and looked into his face, automatically reaching for his wrist and checking the pulse. His eyes only closed for the moment of the faint, then fluttered open again. He seemed to wonder for orientation.

"Welcome to Padua University," Asrian supplied, smiling. "You just took faint."

She pulled up his eyelids and opened his mouth with her fingers. He regained his composure in a moment and waved her away from these actions.

"Thank you, I'm fine. Really, I'm fine now. It's all right; I am a student of medicine."

"Ho, ho! Then, there is nothing that could go wrong with you."

He smiled slightly at the rebuff and allowed her to finish taking his pulse.

"I'll stand now." Asrian held on to him as he rose to his feet. He blinked a bit impatiently and turned to her. "Thank you."

He began to walk away. He had walked probably forty feet and took the next exit, walking into the sun and taking several deep breaths. He had wandered into a small sitting garden, and found a bench now, nestled in some tall yellow rose bushes. He turned his face to the sun and closed his eyes, feeling the full warmth of the light on his skin. He stayed this way for several more deep breaths, then, refreshed, opened his eyes. Asrian was beside him.

"Sir, I thank you for your intercession and your concern,

but I am quite fine now, and thank you."

Asrian smiled. "Lovely gardens, aren't these?"

He sighed with irritation. "Yes, they are."

"Were you sick, then?"

His eyes opened wide on the bushes before them. "Yes sir, I was. I am on recovery. But I am well now."

"Are you new here, then?"

William's voice was growing more and more rigid and formal. "Yes. I studied at Gonville and Cais College, Cambridge beginning in 1593, received my B.A. in '97, and was ill most of the period between '98 and '99. Now I am beginning study here at Padua. Are all students here as forward as you?"

"Oh no. You've been fortunate. I am one of the most forward and engaging fellows in the whole university. Pleasure to meet you. My name is Asrian." She held out her hand. He regarded her with a cold stare, looking straight into her black eyes. Perhaps it was the childlike openness of her smile, or the exuberant humor in her eyes; whatever, he could not hold the coldness and broke into a grin. They shook hands.

"You're English," she said.

"Yes, born in Kent. Haven't been out of England long."

"I thought you were English as soon as I saw you. Well, you're not Italian, that's plain. You'll love the anatomy theater here. Have you seen it?"

"Yes, actually, I have attended a few lectures there. A very intriguing approach, the lecture using dissection for illustration. I'm quite enjoying that aspect of the university already. Are you a student of medicine also?"

"I have been here long enough to have a hard look at most all subjects."

"How long is that?"

She fixed her black eyes on him. "Nearly twenty years." She laughed at his expression, knowing that she had probably been at Padua for as long as he had been alive. "Out of choice. And no, I do not teach. I am a student. I consider myself an accomplished man of the Renaissance, with a full love of the classics, literature as a whole, and art and music, but my passion is the sciences."

"Which?"

"All of them." She turned to him as if to whisper a great secret. "I shouldn't say so soon upon meeting you, but they're all the same."

William stifled a smile at her manner and held his eyes wide to convey seriousness.

"How so, the same?"

Thus was the beginning of what would prove to be the strongest friendship of both their lives.

~

They began meeting often, William realizing that his new friend had been in the university so long and was so impressive as a scholar that he could learn much from him about the subjects as well as about the university. They continued their discussions whenever possible, through the halls of the studium, on the streets of the town. In art galleries they would begin to inspect the artwork, and in a matter of minutes the glint in a painted eye, or the tiny winged cherubim, or the shine of a bronze frame would somehow revert them to discussing their studies. William was inseparable from his eggs and embryos; Asrian's mind stretched so constantly over all the matters she could possibly encompass, that not infrequently there would fall long silences between them, each lost in his own thoughts. Peers made a joke of the scenario so often observed between them, such draughts of silence, and then one suddenly rousing the other with a sudden thought spoken aloud, the rousing of one waking suddenly from a deep sleep.

Asrian's pursuit of knowledge ran all the paths she met: astronomy, astrology, optics, herbs, nature studies, rhetoric, logic, mathematics, grammar, and so on until she could grasp at parallel concepts like grabbing up the corners of a blanket, and folding it over itself until the wonders of the world were contained in one uniting philosophy. This was her vision, this combining of the sciences, intertwining the laws of nature, mapping out of every seemingly small and stray discovery so that the universal laws could be articulated and understood. For just as William's studies were showing all early lifeforms as being similar, so must all laws and processes ultimately resemble basic governing principles.

They talked excitedly through the late hours of the night, staying on at the University for as long as possible, and then continuing over dinner, and generally into William's modest room, the room of any young student in all regards except that he kept a secret stock of hens and roosters for study. Asrian was delighted with her friend's eccentricity, and moreover, his fervor.

William reached beneath a hen and extracted, much to its irritation, a new egg. He placed it in Asrian's palm.

"Take note of the pulse." He reached onto the windowsill and withdrew an egg which had been sitting on it.

"This egg has been setting exposed to the cold. Take note of its pulse."

She held the two eggs in either hand. "The cold egg registers a slower pulse rate."

He replaced the eggs appropriately, nodding in approval. "The egg without the warmth of incubation suffers considerably, its heartbeat growing slower even to the threat of death." He waited a moment. "Now the heartbeat will have ceased completely, so that the egg is completely devoid of any signs of life. But here, lay a finger on its shell."

She looked carefully at the egg, with the focus that denotes concentration of any sense other than sight. She cocked her head toward him. "It's coming back."

An excited grin spread on his face. "Within twenty beats of my pulse, the little heart is revived. Lo! It returns from the very edge of death."

"Is it the influence of my pulse?"

"Not exclusively," he answered. "The same result is achieved through the application of heat by any means—a flame, hot water or any liquid. It is the heat itself from which the heart draws its power, the power necessary for life. Not that the heat is imbued with any life-instilling properties, for heat applied to a rock or any other otherwise inanimate object does not infuse it with life. The embryo possesses, even in its weakened state, the enormous power to draw life into itself. The embryo is a staggering mystery.

"And yet, for all its strength, the chick *in ovo* is of a most delicate constitution; Aristotle observed that 'Eggs are spoiled and become addled in warm weather. . . . When it thunders, the eggs that are under incubation are spoiled.'"

She opened her wide hands. "Thus it is that eggs that have rotted during the high months are termed *cynosura*, and further that Columella states 'the summer solstice, in the opinion of many, is not a good season for breeding chickens.'" Here eyes riverted to the egg on the sill. "What day is it in?"

"Its third day, and three nights as well, " he answered.

"Aristotle recorded traces of generation in the egg at this juncture."

"Yes," he nodded again. "So he did. As did Fabricus. A critical day, this. Tomorrow even more so." He bent down to the egg. "Tomorrow the center will show a tiny spot of palpitating red—the first blood of its life—in the diffluent fluid, the spot so slight to the naked eye that as it contracts, it disappears, and when the yolk dialates again, it flares red like the smallest spark of fire."

"This, then, is the beginning of its true animal lifetime."

His eyes met hers when she said this, and they held gazes of profound significance. Asrian walked to the sill, lifted the egg, and placed it beneath the hen, which squawked in indignation.

They walked in like rhythm in the bright light of the sun, Asrian swinging her arms back and forth, William staring straight ahead.

"What is so astounding in early lifeforms is their simple similarity, the rudiments of all animals nearly always appearing like the maggot. This is the case in the dog, the horse, the deer, the fowl, the snake—"

"Man," she interjected. "What this would indicate is that they all have common appearance in origin, for these early creatures would not, in all logic, begin with drastic differences, and then similarize, and then branch off again. That all would undergo a stage of resemblance at parallel times in their development is an indication in itself that they have to this point been similar, especially granted the simplicity of the life form in question, the maggot. What could be simpler and therefore precede such a simplicity?"

Students passed them, their gowns flowing over their movements. "Yes, I agree utterly. Essential logic. But the first stage is too small to be observed. Again, Aristotle had noted the same, as in his statement, 'In all, even those that lay perfect eggs, the first conception grows while it is yet invisible; and this, too, is the nature of the worm.' But he is flawed when he speaks in connection with this as spontaneous generation, for, as you note, it is not logical for life to evolve in varied forms of origin and suddenly assume a common form. Aristotle spoke of those insects which were born of the dew on leaves and blades of grass. Yet these same insects will develop into the maggot-like pupae at some stage, in some cases indefinitely.

"Therefore, granted that all life forms do begin in like, what is their original form? At what point can it be altered or influenced?"

"How could it be influenced, William? Is it possible? But first and important in its own right, what is the common original form? All creatures generate from the womb. The answer lies therein."

On and on their studies and discussions went, reading the treatises on surgery by Bruno do Longoburgo, studying extensively the works of eminent Paduan medical students, Dino del Garbo and Gentile do Foligno and their famous teacher Peter of Abano. They poured for hours over the weighty *Grabadin* by Peter of Abano, the standard western European reference pharmacopoeia and supplement of complaints concerning the heart and digestive system. Peter had set the precedent of thinking medicine and philosophy sisters, claiming the science of medicine was outstanding among the arts because it was of superlative usefulness and truly necessary, and attracted honor, friendship, and prosperity to its students. Padua stressed this relationship of medicine and philosophy, both in and of themselves being cultivated arts as well as sciences.

Together they worked through the Greek and Arab contributions to herbal remedy, from obscure scripts filed in the libraries to the standard collection of Jacopo Dondi. They kept abreast of Bacon's publications, each possessing the recent Latin text *Essays*. ("He writes about science like a Lord Chancellor," William told Asrian.) They pursued current developments such as the scientific method and inductive logic applications, as well as absorbing all they could of the classics. They quizzed one another often on their retention of and prolific citing from the revered works of the great philosopher, Aristotle, studying constantly the invaluable treatises that had survived time in tangibility and ideology: *Libri Naturales, Physica, Metaphysica, De Anima, Parva Naturalia, Historia Animalium,* and on. These treatises were their very pith of thought, and they discussed them tirelessly. Armed with the ideas and studies of ages, their sharp minds would begin bridging discoveries, and inspiring pursuits of their own.

"I want to study a woman, Asrian."

Asrian's eyes kept moving back and forth across the

page she was reading. "Then you study a woman, William," she mumbled.

He raised his eyes in thought. "I need to see her uterus."

"Well, William, they go at a price."

"Hmm?"

Asrian looked at him. "How soon do you want her?"

"Soon, as soon as possible."

She rose and closed her book. "Put on a fresh shirt and look smart. We're going to find you a woman."

They walked into the night air. Asrian drew a deep breath of it through her nostrils. "Now, this is what we should be doing more often than we are. This sort of stretch clears the mind and restores the muscles. How are you feeling?"

He lengthened his strides to keep up with Asrian's. "Fine. Where are you getting me a woman from?"

She put her arm around his shoulders. "If you walked an hour like this every evening for a month, I guarantee you, you would feel a completely different person."

"I plan on doing that tonight. Are you getting me one who's fertile? I need one who's fertile."

"Myself, I wouldn't miss my daily exercise. Part of the new thinking, William. All the humanists know it—riding, fencing, hunting, you choose one or all, and it is an instant commitment to feeling better and becoming a more rounded person. Greeks knew it."

"Asrian . . ."

"Ssh! Look." She stood still, and he followed suit, trying to see what she was looking at. The evening district was alive and well, gentlemen wearing their finer gowns of puffed sleeves, lights burning with the promise of drink, laughter welling from the open windows. In a slight alcove that lay between two buildings, a flare of color rustled, revealing the pale faces of two painted women. They laughed and winked coyly at Asrian and William. William nodded politely back and turned his face in to Asrian, grabbing her by the neck.

144

"Are you mad? You can't possibly think that—"

Asrian smiled broadly over his shoulder at the women. "Now, now, William. You are looking for a body, and these are businesswomen with just that to sell. It's perfectly logical." She kept grinning their way.

"They expect a man only so far inside!"

"Come, my friend, you are squandering your resources. Watch."

Asrian broke away and walked over to the alcove. William fumed, standing alone on the walk, looking up and down the street. The women were laughing loudly. One called "Willy!" in a high-pitched voice. William turned his back and pulled his collar closer to his neck. Then they fell quiet, and several minutes passed. William eventually moved his head just slightly over his shoulder to glance behind, and then shuffled his foot and finally faced them. Asrian was talking steadily, not moving her hands or head. They appeared to be listening quite gravely. Then the light-haired younger one of the two cocked her head completely to one side in the attitude of an Irish Wolfhound, and bounded off determinedly down the alleyway. The older woman, however, continued to give her attention to Asrian's tall and handsome form. He finished what he was saying at last, and she nodded, slowly at first, and then more quickly. They turned and walked toward William. He studied the placement of his feet.

"William, meet Eliza. She is going to be your research body."

William made a stiff smile which fell. She grinned politely and easily, a pretty woman of probably the same age as Asrian. He smiled again, more strongly this time, and offered her his hand.

"All right, we haven't got all night," Asrian announced. "Let's get to work."

"Closer."

Asrian moved the lantern nearer the incision, the light shining on William's tied tail of hair curling down his back.

"That's better. You see, Asrian, this ovary is plump. She is due to begin menstruation any time now."

The woman murmured. Asrian reached the bottle of spirits to her with his free hand, pouring it sloppily over her slack lips.

"Is it a healthy ovary?"

William's voice was low with concentration. "From what I can tell, yes. Bear in mind that I have never seen a live human ovary before . . ."

The silver instruments glinted in the light of the lantern.

"I am sure . . . that this is what we're looking for." His arm moved slowly. "This . . . is . . . certainly it." He pulled the silver instrument away from the body, narrowing his eyes as he examined its matter.

"Yes? Yes?" The light flickered with Asrian's movement. "An egg?"

William looked at Asrian with an expression of triumph.

"A human egg."

⬎

William set down his notebook with a smack that startled Asrian into wakefulness, jerking up from her slump at his desk.

"Morning." She said through closed eyes.

"Good morning. Wake up, you have the future of science before you."

Asrian blinked. William's hair was coming loose from its tie. The sun had risen at some point.

"Now listen. The first time these words are being spoken." William splayed his hand on his notes. "It appears that the rudiments of the eggs in the ovary are of very small size, mere specks, smaller than millet seed, white and replete with watery fluid. These specks, however, by and by, must become yolks, and then surround themselves with albumen. This is the same pattern followed by all animals I have examined to date. you know what this means?"

"We're having eggs for breakfast."

"It means, Asrian, that we have just made possibly the most significant discovery in all of animal science: *Omne animal est ex ovo;* every animal is from the egg. "

⁓

"William, I must have the largest supper ever consumed by man, and I must have it now!" The door swung closed behind her. William rose from his desk and took Asrian by the arm, guiding her to sit.

"Asrian. Which came first, the chicken or the egg?" Asrian blinked. "The egg is older than the fowl, the fowl having been produced from it, and, on the contrary, this fowl existed before that egg, which she has laid. Now we see inherent in this timeless question, sported with by Plutarch, a basic assumption: only one fowl was involved in the conception of said egg, and this fowl was involved in the conception of said egg, and this fowl was female. The theory of female autoreproduction stands on equal footing with either solution, for, be it the egg precedes the hen, then it is the creature within the egg which perpetuates itself, and if, on the other hand, the hen is the original, then it is she who produces the fertilized egg within herself.

Consider this: Aristotle tells us in the *History of Animals* that in Persia, it has been discovered, on cutting open the female mouse, that the young ones contained in the belly are already pregnant; in other words, they are mothers before they are even born!"

"Yes, I remember."

William moved in a way that reminded Asria of the Scottish snap.

"Don't you see what this means? What it makes possible?

What it suggests?"

"Does it suggest something we can discuss over supper?"

~

The bread and cheese laid half-touched on the desk. William was moving animatedly through his little hen-coup.

"According to Aristotle, in the world at large it is admitted that the earth is to nature as the female or mother, while climate, the sun, and other things of the same description, are spoken of by the names of generator and father. The earth, too, spontaneously engenders many things without seed; and among animals, certain females, but females only, procreate of themselves and without the concurrence of the male: hens, for example, lay hyperemic eggs; but males, without the intervention of females, engender nothing.

"This egg was laid without the aid of a male. This egg is the product of an undefiled hen."

"But it is not fertilized," Asrian said, following his pacing with her eyes.

"No, it is not. But this is only one egg, one in all the eggs of all hens, and of all the species of birds of the world."

"And egg-laying mammals," She interjected.

"Which is not a qualification."

"Never dreamt it was."

He strode on. "But why did the hen lay an egg of her own accord? What was the process? What can we do with this egg now that we have it?"

"Record it. Record it with the thoroughness you always do."

"Yes." He stared at it.

"Solemn warning, I give to you now: some of the biggest mistakes in scientific research have occurred because of simple oversight in excitement."

William nodded, still eyeing the egg. "And in all other areas of life, I should think."

"Universal law . . ." Asrian's voice trailed off, and William looked at her suddenly.

"I am sorry, you have studies of your own you should be working on. Am I keeping you?"

She roused herself from her musing. "What? No, no, you're not. On the contrary, your research feeds into my master argument, as it of course must." She laughed to herself. "Besides, my research is at a stage of steady observation and recording; taking in of information rather than creating new and putting it out. You have your examination in less than two months."

"Yes," he answered, his stare moving over the hens. "And you know what thesis I propose to argue."

"I do. Let me be the first to toast your discoveries."

She poured them both tall glasses of wine, and he moved as if reminded to resume eating their quick meal of the bread and the cheese. She touched the top of her glass to the bottom of his.

⌒

The next two months were intense research in preparation for William's master's thesis. Asrian brought William a new fowl, smuggling it in under her coat, her cough a red herring as she hurried up the stairwell. Wick after wick was burned through the nights, ink pots emptying under their driven hands. Pages filled as each copied the notes of the other, drawing from and contributing to the other's research as fit. The pages were crammed with not only words, but sketches, Asria having drawn her own version of Copernicus' circular orbits of the nine planets of the solar system, countless herbs, trees, and plants of all sorts, both from study and oral description she gleaned from foreigners, and page after page of biological drawings. Not even sixty years ago Vesalius had given the world his inspired anatomical drawings, and William and Asria kept them posted about now. There was the careful drawing of a skeleton contemplating a skull, the skull being a symbol of death. Each bone was so meticulously positioned, each bend of the extremities so precise, that Asria's mind played tricks with the picture, infusing the figure with life, clothing it with skin, lending expression to the featureless face on the animate skeleton. His figures were all like this, *Fabrica* an elegant portrayal of a skeleton walking, its profile completely natural in the curves of motion. The right arm pointed downward, the left reaching up in a dancer's arc, the tilt of the "face" gracefully following its line toward the heavens.

They kept all their notes in Latin, thinking English likely too transient to endure. Hebrew was offered, and Asria immediately enrolled, finding foreign languages easy and unintrusive additions to make to her learning. They combed again through all of the famous medical texts that they could, marking down this line and that passage where it may contribute to William's theory. It was bigger than the common origin of the egg, Asria knew. It was growing daily, and they grew so excited in their research that neither one seemed to sleep a night through anymore. Asria seemed to move in by happenstance, the shifts of egg and hen observation and recording dividing between the two of them. One would fall asleep against a wall or over the desk, the other picking up the log and carrying on where the notes left off.

The weeks passed without their knowing. The pages piled and the refining began, organization of the bits and pieces of information forming a cohesive, orderly written thesis. The night before the exam, Asrian insisted on sleep.

"Your work is complete. You will need all of your faculties fresh and at your command tomorrow. No midnight oil tonight."

William conceded, and the candle was blown out.

⌒

Asrian saw to a huge breakfast, which William argued was excessive and lavish. She wiped her chin.

"I will be working in the library while you are in your exam. I'll find you afterward."

"I don't know how long I will be ..."

"As long it takes."

William nodded and ate heartily.

❧

William glanced at the scholars. He fingered his notes and cleared his throat a bit. The hall was silent, and his head was a little light with the utter focus of attention of his superiors on him. He waited for the clock to tick onto the exact time of his examination, and began to speak.

❧

In the library, Asrian walked up and down the rows of books. She had heard it rumored that the University might install a rotating bookcase, the sort that turned its shelves on great wheels by cranking a handle. She hummphed under her breath, creating the vision in her mind, and thinking how cumbersome and wasteful of space such furniture would be. A fashion of the rich, he thought. It will pass.

Books were added to the library constantly, new translations of the Arab and Greek manuscripts, and all the classics she had known for so long coming in illustrious print and tight binding. Long strides from the days of scrolls and leaves bound together. She rubbed her finger on one of the new bindings. She sat down to a copy of new English poetry. Lot of paper space gone to those margins, she thought. She stared at the cover and wondered if William had remembered his entire introduction.

❧

William's voice was authoritative and clear.

"Aristotle, among the ancients, and Hieronymus Fabricus of Aquapendente, among the moderns, have written with so much accuracy on the generation and formation of the egg that little seems left for others to do. Ulyssus Aldrovandus, nevertheless, described the formation of the chick in ovo; but he appears to have gone by the guidance of Aristotle than to have relied on his own experience. For Volcherus Coiter, living at this time in Bologna, and encouraged, as he tells us, by Aldrovandus, his master, opened incubated eggs every day, and illustrated many points besides those noted by Aldrovandus; these discovered, however, could scarcely have remained unknown to Aldrovandus. Emilius Parisanus, a Venetian physician, having discarded the opinions of others, has also given a new account of the formation of the chick from the egg." William looked from his audience to his notes.

＊

The library was silent, except for the occasional whisper or cleared throat. Asrian tapped her fingers on the closed book of poetry in an oblivious mounting rhythm, steady and constant, until a boy looked at her sharply. She smiled and laid her other hand over the autonomous one. She checked the time. William had been in his exam for over an hour.

＊

"Does copulation in fact bear any relevance to fertilization?" William asked his audience. "In looking to the fowl, sufficient evidence exists to reasonably question the connection, perhaps extinguish the contingency entirely. The cock does not possess a penis, although he does appear to follow all the courting and copulation ritual of other fowl who possess such, as the goose and the duck. The orifices of the male and female cloaca tense and project at the height of the ritual; however, I do not believe that the organs of the male enter the female at all. Fabricus affirms that the seed of the cock ejected in coition never does, nor can, enter the cavity of the womb, where the egg is formed.

The theory wanders pale and in want of fortification that throughout nature, the male properly initiates desire within the female, leads her through courtship, and subsequently causes her to produce eggs. No substantiation, furthermore, can be given to those who claim that, in order for impregnation to be successful, the penis must act as an injecting valve dispatching semen into the female, which is absorbed by the corresponding receptacle of the female, namely, the vagina and/or uterus. For, in the copulation of horses, dogs, cats, birds, and other creatures, it is the female who presents her hardened and projecting organ to the male.

Consider this matter in birds. The impassioned bird will present her uterine orifice for stimulation. If this organ is stimulated by the brush of a human finger, she will produce eggs. Aristotle observed the same. This production would appear to be the direct result of the desire and passion of the female only, as my experiments and observations have shown. "I have seen a single hen-pheasant shut up with a cock-bird (which she could in no way escape) so worn out, and her back so entirely stripped of feathers through his reiterated assaults, that at length she died exhausted. In the body of this bird, however, I did not discover even the rudiments of eggs." So the production of eggs is the direct result exclusively of the arousal and desire of the female, and not influenced by the degree of passion of the male at all.

This fact being established, the next and crucial question is this: how does the egg become fertilized? There is no difference whatever between the barren and the fruitful egg. Nor does there exist any indication that the seminal fluid dispatched by the male has entered the uterus or contacted the egg. Nevertheless, the eggs we have observed to date all indicate that the presence of the male's semen results, albeit a time after contact, in the fertilization of the egg.

This semen does not enter the egg. I myself have tried every manner of probe, point, and bristle to penetrate the shell, yet even beneath the eyes of the ray, it remains perfect and wholly, defensively, intact. So the concept of the semen interacting with the contents of the egg must be dispelled as no more than myth. Here enters the mysterious sexuality of the female body, pointedly, menstruation. The uterus, warmed by arousal, draws moisture and the coursing of blood, as corresponds in the engorged and wetting penis of the male. The organ of the female, however, being essentially an internal organ, whether extruded at the moment or not, has not the tightly woven skin of the superficial penis, and so fluid and air may pass through the membrane into and out of the body. Thus escapes the blood of menstruation, gathered and settled in the superior uterus, rendered, through its settlement, ineffective and superfluous. According to the pitch of arousal which originally drew and trapped the blood, the uterus will discharge the blood gradually, even over a period of days, so that, as the blood sits in wait of escape, it may become viscous and coagulate, discharge ranging from normal bloodflow consistency to fluid more of a mucus thickness, to clots. If this overspill of blood is not allowed to escape, it will rot in the body, infecting the internals of the female. This procrastination of the discharge results, therefore, throughout the menstruation process, in cramping, appetite upset, tiredness, listlessness, and distraction, and were it to remain indefinitely, would logically result in death.

So how comes the fertilization? Aristotle stated, 'We call that animal male which engenders in another, female that which engenders itself.' My own opinion is that the semen of the cock thrown into the commencement of the uterus, produces an influence on the whole of the uterus, and at the same time renders fruitful" the egg; "and this the semen effects by its peculiar property or *irradiative spirituous substance*.

That this influence, ipso facto, can be generated only by the male, is immediately apparent as ludicrous. Where lies the evidence for this? Granted, on the whole, the female mind is known to be inferior to the male, as she demonstrates inferior yearning or faculty to learn, and is better suited to duties of coordination of the body, which can be learned easily, such as the duties of the house. But she is capable of learning such coordination, and this trick with nature, the influence of the spirituous substance, is a specific coordination. So stands it not as obvious that this activity is simply a matter of learning, necessitating only proper exposure to and teaching of lessons? Therefore, this matter of transmitting the mental messages to the egg which produce fertilization is at base a technique and a practice which can be taught from the male mind, in which the spirituous influence is inherent and largely unconscious, to the female mind, whereupon it may be memorized, replicated, and the same results obtained. Namely, the female is without need of the male for reproduction."

William was startled by the undeniable murmur of amusement from the scholars. He looked up. These were not the faces of studiously engaged men. A lecturer in the second row grinned at him broadly. He looked down at his notes and began his formal conclusion.

The exam ended finally, and William left the hall quickly, tucking his notes securely under his arm. The judging conference was closed to him, and he hadn't heard a word, but his feet were cursedly slow to carry him to his room, and his head was a bit weak. He held his notes tightly to his middle to brace the rumbling of his stomach. He was not hungry.

⁀

If the male can teach the female his precise mental sensation that he experiences at the moment of fertilization, namely, the orgasm, then she can duplicate the experience and fertilize the egg herself. The concept is simple in essence, thought William as he poured more oil into the lamp. A technique is no more than a specialized coordination. He opened his notes on the progress of the eggs and set his pen to the page. There was a knock at the door.

"William? Is it too late? I know you are not asleep."

It was Asrian's voice.

"Let yourself in," William mumbled. "You have a key." Asrian knocked again. He grunted and got to his feet. He stood too quickly, hitting his head on the low-hanging beam, and wincing, opened the door.

"Hello, Asrian. Certainly not too late for you. Come in."

She hung her overcoat with his, drawing from it as she did so a full bottle of wine.

"The nectar of Bacchus, William! I bring you the finest of tastes of all of Italy."

"You are too kind."

Asrian leaned with her back against the wall to open the bottle, her leg propped on his chair. She worked off the cork and threw it to him. He caught it.

"Glasses or no?"

William looked at a loss.

"Nevermind then. Drink."

William took a nearby chair, pulling it up to the desk, so as not to disturb Asrian. He drank some of the wine, his brow smooth with the distraction of his company, and drank some more. They talked lightly of how warm the day had been, and then fell quiet. The pause drew on. She stared evenly at him.

"I'm sorry," She said.

"They thought it was absurd." His voice was flat.

"I know."

The lamp burned on through the night, the oil which he had replaced growing into blue and orange flame. They talked thinly. Asrian exhausted the weaknesses of each scholar who had been present at William's examination and encouraged him to do the same. He had not the vitality to join in but nearly smiled at Asrian's more outrageous remarks. When the bottle was finished, they sat before it, in their intoxicated silence looking stunned, both staring straight into the flame.

William's voice was slow.

"You know, Asrian, I really believe it."

Asrian looked at him and back at the flame. "I know, William. I do too."

His eyes reflected the light with the shine of glass, his brows arched to punctuate his thinking. "All I have seen and all I have reasoned is sound, comprehensive logic. They will not always laugh at this. Another will come, one perhaps, who has a more convincing tongue or more money for research . . ."

The glow touched her cheek in the otherwise dark room. William's notes were still before them. "What you have found is new ground, my friend. The world is harsh to those who would challenge its comfortable beliefs. Change is slow."

"Strides are being make in science all the time."

"These are strides built upon established truths. Little, if anything, is actually challenged. What you propose is revolutionary to established thought."

"I want only to share my findings. I work in service to the scientific world, not against it."

Asrian's back snapped rigid. "There now. This is exactly the sort of thing to interfere with your studies. You must, above all things, remain clear, or you cannot be of service to yourself or anyone else."

There was a silence.

"Of course you are right, Asrian. You hold more wisdom in these matters than I. You have seen more of life. I suppose this is simply the breaking of the delusions of youth."

She smiled politely, and they were silent again. Finally, Asrian spoke.

"No matter how well constructed your argument is, no matter how true the content, the world will not listen to you without evidence people can see and touch. They want it here." She held out her hand, striking the palm with the back of her other hand. "It is a pity to the outside world that they must endure the intangible words of any explanation. The sorting and the processing of abstract concepts in speeches and in arguments and letters and books is a chore to the majority, William. People want, as any theatre knows, one hell of a spectacle which gives them all the feelings of being intellectual without any of the actual work. In their most serious moments, they still want to be entertained. Instead of the well-formed argument, give them a monster in a cage. They'll be all yours, and your words will pass as law. And who knows? At that point, some of them may even listen to you."

He looked at her in the half-light of the oil lamp. His hair framed his eyes.

"Where am I going to find a willing virgin female?"

*

"The male and the female by themselves, and separately, are not potentially reproductive, but become so united *in coitu*, and made one animal, as it were: whence, from the two as one, is produced and educed that which is the true efficient proximate cause of conception." Asrian showed him the passage in their early notes. He looked at it carefully, one hand still holding a flapping hen. He nodded.

"Which translates, in the theory of autoreproduction, to imprinting of the essence of the genitor."

"Meaning that the mother who fertilizes her own egg can pass on her own qualities, and magnify them in the offspring," Asrian said.

"Exactly. The implications for this are twofold." He clipped more of the wing. The hen squawked. "One, as the generations succeed, the dominant qualities they inherit will grow stronger, each mother furthering the same qualities without interference of foreign qualities from a male."

"The line is pure."

"Yes. This all results in eventual quintessence of the original qualities."

Asrian looked up from her writing and took note of which

hen William was on. "A hawk that could see Saturn."

William laughed. "In fact, that's not out of proportion. But there is no telling how long the super-powered offspring would take to be produced."

He replaced the hen and drew out the next one.

"And the other implication?" asked Asrian.

"Oh yes. The other implication is that if this process of fertilization is a cerebral one, then so too may be the selection of these qualities."

Asrian nodded. "It is logical. Even if it is not practiced now, that does not eliminate the possibility." She mused. "But is it not practiced? What is going on in the mind of the male at the moment of conception?"

"Nothing lucid."

"No, but then the seeds of thoughts are not lucid. Thoughts are articulated only through an arbitrary practice, the practice of language. Before a word is applied to a thought, it is still a thought. This is why so often the precise word cannot be found to convey one's thoughts. This is why, for example, English is forever adopting foreign words."

"Yes, I see your point." William muttered in fascination. "So the question, as it always is, is what happens in the mind during conception?"

Asrian looked absently at the hen William was clipping. "Well, what have you found?"

William slipped the clippers and the hen cried out. "Pardon?"

She cleared her throat. "I mean, what has gone through your mind at . . . such times?"

He grew intent on the wing he was working on. "Well, Asrian, I . . . to tell you the truth, I have spent most of my young life up at university; and, for a year, anyway, ill, and . . ."

She nodded. "I see."

"And you?" He looked at her.

"Me what?"

"You're a man of years and experience. What have you found . . . at such times?"

Asrian stared at the hen. "I think you better turn that wing out a bit."

"Oh, right." The clippers clipped.

Asrian dipped her pen in ink. "Well, William, it has been my experience that, well, that . . ." He looked at her. "It has not been my experience."

"Mmhmm." William assented lightly. They finished the birds and measured out their grain.

"Well, I suppose we need to interview men," William said.

"Interview nothing." Asrian held the heavy sack of seed as William adjusted the funnel.

"Pardon?"

"You know we can't interview," she said. "Any account we get will only be secondhand, hearsay, more thoughts possibly misaptly translated into words, potentially misconstrued by us, hence incorrectly applied in experiment, and consequently hindering research to an inestimable degree. This is not a matter on which we can rely on another's description."

There was a pause. Then William spoke. "Well, Asrian, you are the older and more worldly one of us two, and frankly—"

The grain spilled over the funnel and onto the floor. Asrian yanked the sack back up.

"Frankly, William, I . . . " Her voice tapered off. She looked him square in the face. "There is something about me, William. It is something private, something I have never told . . . anyone."

William's young eyes widened. "Are you homosexual, then?"

"No! Not at all!"

"Of course not," Harvey overlapped. "I never thought for a minute . . . "

"No, no I'm not." Asrian's eyes met his. "But I do have a secret, and I suppose now I must tell you." He waited. Asrian

160

took a deep breath and searched her eyes around the small room. She looked at him again. "William, you have been a good friend to me, and it would be dishonest of me to with hold the truth from you now. I have held this secret for a long time, and it would probably relieve me to share it with someone anyhow." They stared at each other. "William, I am impotent."

William turned to cleaning the seed up off the floor. Asrian hurried to help. They cleared up the spill and fed the chickens without another word. They stood side by side before the pecking hens.

"Well then," said William. "I guess it's up to me."

⌒

"Not a thing to be worried about," said Asrian as they walked down the street.

"I'm glad you're so confident," he replied tersely. The smell of ale and the city was strong on the night air. "How do I look?"

"Just fine," Asrian said without a glance. "Remember, just do what you must."

William grimaced.

"There we go," her voice raised. She put her arm over his shoulders. "Bolster up, boy; be brave. It had to happen sooner or later." A small cluster of evening ladies smiled and waved in their direction. Asrian ushered William toward them. "Not a thing to be worried about. These are professionals."

William's feet suddenly froze. "You'll be here when I'm through?"

"Certainly. Now, let's get you suited up. Which do you suppose—"

"But Asrian, I can't do this. What happens when she becomes pregnant?"

She pushed him forward. "That is precisely what we are going to find out." She stepped up to the group. William's

161

face blanched.

"Evening, ladies," Asrian's voice was smooth. *A true gentleman*, William thought. *Asrian could do anything.*

"Evening," one of them said in street Italian. Her cheeks were impossibly pink. "Feeling a bit cold outside? Looking for something to . . . warm you up?"

Another woman shoved her aside. "What she means is, do you want to be warmed up or put into heat?" William tried to turn his back to the street.

"Well now, such inviting offers all, but it's not for me. It's a present, for my son here."

William's mouth dropped. The second woman smiled at him. "That's a father getting his son a proper education. How old you up to now?"

He spoke, but his voice started too high and cracked. He coughed and began again. "Fifteen, ma'am." She laughed and ruffled his hair with her fingers. He cocked his head into his collar.

"Father," he articulated pointedly, "Don't you think I should be getting on with this so that I am home in time for supper? Mother will be worried."

Asrian worked out the arrangements with the woman and paid her. She put her hand on his shoulder. "Son, you're going in there a boy. I want you to know that when you come out, you'll still be a boy." William boxed her on the arm and turned infuriated into the open doorway. Asrian wandered down the street, laughing in the open air.

An hour later, the door opened, and William staggered outside. A long white arm set him on the street.

"Goodbye, Willie, and do come back!" The door closed.

Asrian waited. "Well? Was it successful?" William didn't move. "William, wipe that grin off, for heaven sake, you look like a perfect idiot."

William turned to her, his face flushed and shiny.

"Well?" Asrian demanded.

He blinked. "I think I should do it again to be sure."

⁓

"Just pleasure."

"Nothing else?"

William drank more wine.

"Nothing lucid."

Asrian waved this away. "We've been through all this. We need to know the sensation. The thoughts behind the poetry and the vulgarity. The base."

He thought a long while. "If there was anything, anything at all beyond pure pleasure, it was the feeling of release."

"Release of?" She pounded on the desk. "It has to be something specific and unique! Otherwise, children would be impregnating their mothers every time they fed them cake!"

William was clearly struggling. "It is not something that language will cover. It is what remains when the pretty verses turn to vapor. It is an overwhelming of sorts, of pleasure, and bliss, and . . ."

"And?" She prompted.

"And . . . love. I didn't know the woman, but in that instant, I loved her, if only as the source of that physical pleasure."

"Now we're getting somewhere." Asrian began to write notes. William sat upright on his bed.

"But all men do not love their women," he continued. "If anyone knows that, those women do."

"I'm not sure I agree with your thinking. If anyone feels desired, which is a form of Eros, if not the romantic form that I presume from your argument which you felt; therefore I say, if anyone feels loved, it is precisely those women."

William shook his head. "You cannot confuse the forms."

Asrian ignored him. "I'm not. But this is irrelevant. The point is that romantic love is not necessary for impregnation. Will you grant that?"

He considered this. "Judging from the oafs I have seen bed

women and cuckolds who have given children to their wives, their mistresses, their whores, and women unwilling—yes."

"So, yes." She scribbled rapidly. "What is necessary is the intense pleasure. Either this is a specific kind of pleasure, or a specific intensity, or both."

"But I loved her! I know that mattered!"

Asrian looked at him sharply. "Please do not expostulate. I stated only that it is not *necessary,* not that it does not influence. I am sure, if you say that it does, then it does. But I think that where this factor figures in is perhaps in the transmitting of qualities that we talked about."

William subdued. "Perhaps he who fertilizes without loving the woman does not pass on his qualities."

Asrian nodded. "Or passes on different ones, poor ones, weakens those he does; who knows? At this point, we can only speculate. But, we can safely say that *what* is absolutely intrinsic to the orgasm?"

He stroked his cheek. "Pleasure. Love: of what form or object, we do not know."

Asrian finished a line of writing and laid her hand on the page. "All right. If that is all we can know, then that is all we can know."

William laid awake in his bed that night, thinking. Asrian had been kind in his conclusion, but he knew that they both knew that they needed to know more. His mind was truly exhausted from laboring over the subject. None of the words he had spoken or thought of now were adequate or appropriate; he couldn't even say which. Yes, he thought, this is precisely the trouble with language. Asrian was right about thoughts and articulation. Well, he reasoned, who was to say that language was the correct means of communication for humans? Who was to say it was the best? If what they were dealing with was a *spiritus* message, then it was inconsistent to try to plug it into words, like putting a square peg in a round hole. Perhaps this had been known. Perhaps this was precisely what poets spoke of when they wrote of the unspoken words between lovers or the anger or sorrow that defies description. He sat upright.

Of course! This was exactly the case! It was so plain, so obvious, what the Germans would term *selbstverständlich*, that he clutched the sides of the bed with self-effacement. So simple. If the matter was not definable by language, then it could not be dealt with through language. It must be met on its own ground. A sudden rapping on his door jolted him. He jumped up and opened it, heart racing. There stood Asrian.

"*Selbstverständlich*," she said.

❧

The night held a chill. The full moon outside provided them with more light than usual to work by. William wrote with wild speed into the notebook.

"How old is the woman?" He asked.

"Forty-five," Asrian answered.

"And you are absolutely certain that she is a virgin?"

"Yes."

"And she is intelligent enough to conduct this experiment?"

"Yes."

"Is she someone you know?"

"Yes," she said quietly. "Very well."

"Is there any repercussion for her if she does fertilize herself?"

"I will concern myself about that."

"Can you entrust her name to me on a sealed paper, with my oath to read it only in the most dire of circumstances?"

"No. I told you that the only way we can conduct this experiment with this woman is through absolute secrecy. I am the only one who is to know her identity."

"And I cannot see her, even to examine her."

"No."

William was tensely silent for a long moment. "All right."

He scribbled more and handed some pages to Asrian. "You must find out all of these things about her. We must have every shred of detail about her that we can possibly get. Add more questions, if they occur to you."

Asrian stood bent over the loose pages, writing on them with her pen.

"I will have all of these answered for you. Tomorrow."

William continued to write more questions. "We must know her medical background, her illness, her constitution, her vitality, and of course, her lineage."

Asrian's pen froze. William noticed and stopped. "What is it?"

An expression fell over Asrian's face that William had never seen before.

"Asrian?"

Her gaze fell to the notes that she had been writing. She spoke softly. "I do not know the lineage."

William caught the note of heaviness in his friend's voice, and respected it with a quieting of his own.

"Can you find out?"

Asrian's eyes remained fixed on the pages. She seemed to be making some decision in her mind. William waited. Suddenly, Asrian turned to him, and spoke with resolution.

"Perhaps there is," she said. She stood erect and set her features into determination. "I will use all of my resources, in the name of knowledge."

William nodded, glad for her apparent peace of decision.

⟨⟩

Asrian bought the necessary tools the next morning. She had a saw, an iron bar with which to pry, and a hammer. That really should do it, she thought. The trunk stood before her as a great unopened door that held in all the spirits of mystery. In a matter of minutes, she thought, my life will be forever changed from what it is now. She sat still in front of

166

it, savoring the thrill and wan sensation. Somewhere came the far sound of laughter, a laughter smaller and lighter than that of children. She gripped her hand round the saw handle and touched the sturdy teeth to the lock.

It was slow going. She had shed some layers of clothing and gained some layers of sweat while only halfway through the lock. The light in the room faded into blue, and she got up, wiping her forehead, and lighted a lamp, placing it down on the floor beside her. Her hands grew sore from the sustained clutch and pressure, and she stopped from time to time to stretch them out. The lock was orange with rust, and her palms stained the same.

Sometime into the night, the saw jerked into the nothingness that told her that she'd realized her goal. She tried it with her hands, and it stuck. She hit it once hard with the hammer, and the lock fell to the floor. She breathed deeply and lifted the lid. The straps gave, and the old stiff hinges yielded to her work. She lifted the lamp.

Inside were packages most securely and carefully packed with cloth. She did not know the type, but it was of a fine weave and did not betray its age. Her fingers worked gently to pry the layers away from the objects within. The topmost item was a document bearing the royal seal of England. She set to it immediately, sliding her knife beneath the wax seal. It was a message of a single line.

This child must never set foot in England.

Beneath the packages was a long exquisite embroidered silk scarf covered with poetry verses in the romance languages and curving pictures of pheasants, snakes, hearts and doves, encrusted with gold throughout, a tribute to Renaissance splendor, shining with rubies, diamonds, emeralds and other precious gems. She touched it gingerly, running her fingers over the jewels, holding her face close to the splendor. Then she set the scarf aside and dug deeper.

The length of the bottom was occupied by rods of iron. They showed more as she cleared away the cloth. She found maps, rolled and bound, of British territories. A bound package lay beneath these. She cut it open. This was a bronze case, simple, very beautifully so, and finely made. The fastening gave without a qualm, and the top slid back without hinges. Inside was a document on extremely unusual paper, paper she could not guess at the fiber of. It belied no wear of age at all, and yet the entire case breathed of antiquity. She stroked the top and set it on the floor close to her.

Now the trunk could be emptied of the packing cloth. She set it neatly in a bundle to her left and lifted the lamp to see inside to the trunk's bottom. The final contents of the trunk were the rods. These iron rods were all connected, she realized, amounting to a Gothic device of considerable craftsmanship which had provided the trunk all of its weight. With some coaxing she lifted it from its place of some forty-odd years, and set it on the floor. It stood roughly waist-high to her on the floor. She decided she had it upside-down and righted it. She examined it carefully, pushing on it this way and that, until—Eureka! It unfolded, a perfect specimen of a fourteenth century curule, a study chair the wealthier and more prominent scholars had used primarily in Italy. The seat was stretched with leather, which she doubted to be its original covering, but was a good idea, as it had enough strength to hold her even now, after all this time in storage. She sat on it with a rush of regal importance, caressing the Gothic claws and turns and twists of the iron. She loved it.

She picked up the bronze case and held it on her lap, balancing the lamp on the open corner of the trunk. The surface was smooth and was in need of polish but gleamed in the light of the flame, even so. The document came easily from its lovely repository, and she marveled again at the paper. The ink was of very fine lines, and completely legible, except that the language was very strange, even to her trained eye. She knew she had a night's work ahead of her.

In fact, it was over a week, but even so, she knew she had made remarkably good time with the translation. She placed it in the older Gaelic origins, with a precision and consistency of grammar which no language today possessed, and a purity of vocabulary that was very impressive indeed. The structures were complex, and took the longest time to decipher. Days later, as she settled into the curule in the brighter moon, with a full oil lamp beside her and a glass of red wine in her hand, she felt comfortable with her translation, and sat back with the prospect of absorbing the final transcription for all of its content, without a thought to its language. She knew her skills enough to be confident in what she'd done. She took a sip of wine and began.

"The core of the witch mania is ignorance. Not one person in my lifetime, varied and worldly as it has been, has been able to satisfactorily answer the question: What is a witch? The perverting of the word and the new stereotype of this fourteenth century are of such influence that the incorrect ideas are bound to persevere hundreds, perhaps even thousands, of years. It is not in my power alone to correct this. Would that it were.

The true witch comes along perhaps once in a century from generations of a strong line. Ordinary humans cannot study and "become" witches. Witches are born with sensitivity to the unseen realm, the countless diverse things that fall clumsily under the heading of 'occult,' meaning 'all things hidden.' Such matters are defined by the seeing world as the congress of thoughts; communication and work wrought by the mind; and trafficking with creatures not usually given to intercourse with humans, creatures given such various interpretations as the little people, the wee folk, elves, faeries, ghosts, goblins, ghouls, spirits, angels, leprechauns, trolls, gnomes, nymphs, sprites, and besides such as these, creatures prevalent and immediate, the like of cats, birds, rodents, and all manner of the worlds of plants and elements. Witches are born with abilities and sensitivities which *must* be dealt with and incorporated in some way. These abilities and sensitivities are as pertinent to them as seeing and hearing are to others.

This is the organism of a witch. Beyond this, the beliefs, the organization, the credos she follows are entirely a question of the individual. I could easily go on about logical paths and progresses their unique qualities lean them toward, but there is little time, and these considerations can be found in my other works.

These so-called students and apprentices, the would-be witches, chase endlessly after bits of knowledge that can only distill into signals and trivia, triggers and techniques of concentration; in other words, they find not the true instruction of being a witch, which is what they seek, for such would be impossible. One can study the techniques of throwing the discus from the finest masters and the most intricate books, but if the student has no arms, it cannot come to fruit. So instead what they acquire is a vast litany of the properties of herbs, names of spirits, procedure of laying tarot cards, the recipes of spells and incantations, descriptions of deities with their various hierarchies, and finally, a false sense of potential within themselves.

The true witch is not anything inherently good nor evil, intelligent nor stupid, knowledgeable nor ignorant, powerful nor weak. The word is a neutral term given to those people born with specific extraordinary faculties. Nothing more, nothing less. Beyond that, the bastardizing of terminology and ideology concerning witchcraft should be dismissed.

Would that I could leave my missive at that and erase the blotting that has begun, and prevent the spill of blackness that once let, will stain the world's minds forever. But I can foresee all too well that these matters which seem so obvious to me now will one day soon need to be explained. And so:

In 1258, the Inquisition posed this question to the Pope: Shouldn't the Church take cognizance of divination and sorcery? Until this point, the question of witchcraft as being linked to devils or in any way blasphemous to Christianity had not even been thought of. The Canon Episcopi declared all belief in witchcraft as heretical, superstitious, admitting faith in something other than God having the power to manipulate and control the natural order of things. One must realize how slow-moving time is to the larger picture of history. Although that idea was put forth a century ago, it moves forth with the freshness of an infant, an infant holding the germ of the Plague.

The sudden suggestion that witchcraft is in opposition to Christianity, and what's more, a perversion of its mythology and terms, has not been accepted easily by even those within the Church. It is rejected utterly. The largest disputer of this new concept is the Catholic theology community itself. I take my place with such traditionalists. I pass as a Catholic theologian, but in fact I have no affiliations whatever and have conducted my theological studies in view of the world as a whole, with no greater or lesser emphasis paid to any creed.

It is now the middle of the fourteenth century. Each Christian religion is claiming to be the only true religion. All unknown beliefs are being branded as Paganism, Heathenism, and Witchcraft. I have come to the conclusion that the term "pagan" is nothing more than vernacular scurrility, laid quickly over such diverse peoples as the Norse, the Franks, the Angles and Saxons, the Prussians, and even indiscriminately any of the Christian peoples, whenever they fall into disgrace with one another. The term becomes more and more interchangeable with barbarian. I shouldn't wonder that linguistic trends will soon melt the two terms into a hybrid, and in the next thousand years, neither will be recognizable on its own. I am disappointed to see the blurring of the lines of my studies, and fear that in with the incorporation of these incorrect ideas, my findings will become obsolete. My years of observation, my journals and tables and charts, may be becoming worthless before my eyes.

For that matter, it is ludicrous that any form of Christianity should assume self-righteousness and supremacy, for Christianity is only a making-over of the Celtic belief system, applying new names to the deities, but borrowing all the mythos and even the calendar. Omniscient and omnipotent Zeus/God the Father, purely begot His god and human son Apollo/Christ, who performed miracles and died at the hands of men.

Certainly more universal and older than the Celt/Christian faith is the religion of the Goddess, the deity Mother revered, by whatever name, as the source of all creation, love, and wrathful judgment. Polytheistic traditions divide her into many goddesses, each with her own individual color and flare.

Myths are fine to examine for their own sakes, but one must never become swept away by a priori. A simple analogy of arithmetic: countless numerical figures exist, with patterns and riddles and astonishing correlations to be drawn therein, but all of these figures are only possible because they are derived from the same original set of numbers and mathematical laws, and it was men who created these numbers and mathematical laws. So it is with religions. But that is another matter.

Having been on the feuding lines of the rising controversy, watching it with the insights of a scholar and an intuitive, I smelled the immense danger of this new controversy even before the first blood flowed. Sareyna, who is my wife, and our daughter last night defected to safety. They have gone home. This is the tiny island of Daculi, just northwest of Ireland and Breasil. The precise location was first mapped for the outside world only in 1320 by Angelino Dulcert and has most recently been marked on the Medici map of 1351, although no outsider has yet approached the island. It is a peaceful, private civilization, populated entirely with our own sprawling lineage. About an eighth the size of Ireland, it hasn't proven large enough to attract any national coveting. The inhabitants are every one of them tremendous thinkers and scholars. Most remain on the island all their lives, devoted to the great study house and library.

Sareyna and I left the island at what are today considered very young ages, devoting our lives to servicing Daculi by study through traveling. We wed only to appease the ethics of the outside world, for on Daculi, there is no marriage. Sareyna was an invaluable companion in travel. Besides speaking several languages, she is a master of dialect, so that as we entered a foreign land, in a matter of hours she could easily pass as a native in any remote pockets of slanted tongue. We moved east through Norway and the Ukraine, along the old silk route through the Gobi desert to the Oriental peoples—with whom we almost settled—west to the Caspian Sea and Cyprus, Crete, Prague with its strange green gems, and all around the Mediterranean, through Egypt, north for what we took to be our last visit home, whereupon I deposited the vast portion of my records then settled slowly down to Rome. Through these years I recorded my studies of belief systems of every society that I came into contact with.

We found, in all our travel, that in fact our tiny island was by far the most intellectually advanced of any of these lands, and I will not expound on that here but refer you to my life's works for examples of this, as well as my conjectured explanations. Our library is certainly superlative, in fact, incomparable, for we are the only land which prints books, and we have been doing so for centuries. We have the most advanced water systems, architecture, and such a clean land I have yet to visit. Although my area of study is prominent, we have never recognized a God and never will. It has always been a clear and quiet haven, a cradle for lovers of learning. In fact, from the word *Daculi* comes the Latin *culla*.

To the point. Sareyna returned. She left for the sake of our young daughter because she felt no compunction to stay through the witch-hunt madness. I have chosen to remain because it interests me. To be in the midst of the storm is to record it with accuracies and details for the archives of Daculi which will otherwise be irretrievably lost. It is that simple. So we bid farewell. I know that was the last I will ever know of them. The parting, to say briefly, was not without pain, but it was with mutual thorough understanding and absolute resolution.

The siege rages on. In 1320, Pope John XXII had issued a bull that allowed the Inquisition at Carcassonne to 'prosecute those who worshiped demons, entered a pact with them, made images, or used sacred objects to work magic.' In ten years, the first trials for heretical sorcery were underway. To date in Carcassonne and Toulouse, 600 people have been burned for heretical witchcraft. Trials are moving throughout the south of France, southern and western Switzerland, into the north of my present home Italy and up into the Rhineland. The entire legal system is shaping itself to these trials and any technological thinking to be done is devoted to crafting new, more heinous devices of torture. As bracing and terrible as this sweep is, opposition is still strong among us traditional theologians. That which the Church had taught not to believe as existing at all is becoming regarded as a heresy to disavow. This idea is already long on its way to just such articulation. I am old now, and Sareyna and my daughter are gone. I do not expect to outlive this storm."

Asrian reexamined the maps that had come from the trunk. They were all maps charting Daculi: the Medici map of 1351, the Pizigani map of 1367, Beccario of 1435, Pareto of 1455. With the maps was a hand-written note in the same pen: 'Italian traders frequently sailed the northern Irish waters and had the island thus brought to light. How its proper name was first discovered by the outside world is unknown.'

Asrian leaned back, closing her eyes and finishing her wine. *I still do not know. I may not ever know. But my origins do not matter to me. I am simply Asria, who passes through the world unseen.* The moonlight showed the rise and fall of her chest slow, and her hand relaxed around the glass. She was asleep.

"The hen, after sexual intercourse, brimful of satisfaction, shakes herself for joy, and, as if already possessed of the richest treasure, as if gifted by supreme Jove, the preserver, with the blessing of fecundity, the hen sets to work to prune and ornament herself. The pigeon, particularly that kind which comes to us from Africa, expresses the satisfaction she feels from intercourse in a remarkable manner; she leaps, spreads her tail, and sweeps the ground with its extremity, and she pecks and prunes her feathers. All her actions are as if she felt raised to the summit of felicity by the gift of fruitfulness. This all means that the process is completed by utter belief in its success. She must celebrate and know all through her being that her womb is full. This is an extension of the bliss known during conception."

Asrian nodded, listening to William with thorough attention. "Beyond that, I end with the same instructions I began with. Make her as comfortable as possible. Keep her warm, provide her with food and water as she wishes, and of course, take painstakingly thorough notes on everything."

"I will," she assured him.

"I know that you will. It is your way." They turned from one corridor into the next, the sun falling cool but bright through the long windows. William stopped and put his hand on Asrian's arm. "I will be in my room all night, reading only. If for whatever reason, you need to see me, a question, or if perhaps something goes wrong . . ."

Asrian put her hand on his. "Thank you, my friend. The experiment will be conducted with the utmost care. I will honor each and every detail in your instruction."

"You have all the notes?"

"Yes. I have them all."

William looked down the corridor. "Well, then, I suppose that is everything."

She wagged her head. "I am sorry, William, that you cannot be there. If there were any other way of doing this—"

He nodded and smiled automatically. "I know. We must do what must be done. This surely will not be the only run of this experiment, and I have utter faith in your abilities, absolutely."

Her voice lowered. "I hope I can do you justice."

"You will, Asrian. Of course you will. You are older and wiser that I." With a sudden impulse, William reached out and embraced her. "I wish you luck." With that, he turned into his lecture hall and was gone.

⁂

Her bed was ringed with candles, tall slender white tapers of beeswax. Sacks of rosemary and rose petals hung about the room, lacing it with heavy perfume. Asrian laid naked on the bed, eyes closed, strong arms dormant at her sides. At the foot of the bed hung the illustration of the female reproductive system that she and William had drawn out, the circles of the ovaries winding long down to the tunnel of the uterus. The wax of the candles dripped and gathered, beading like the beads of sweat that gathered on her skin.

A tiny, white dot floated in the darkness of her inside, or the night sky. She saw it, its outline blurring until it glowed, a dancing speck of light. It swelled and grew, its shape shifting and lengthening. Little veins of brilliant whiteness riddled through its perfect haze, branching out and pushing at the sides of the orb. It broke and the veins fanned through, wavering like a film passing through water. The veins netted and formed wings, the wings fluttering, reaching out of the whiteness, reaching into space, and raising the creature they bore. Tiny features blinked in beauty strange, hair as long as its form swirling out of the orb and filling with the light. Little

176

limbs unfolded, reaching to push the egg away from it, kicking and rising in feisty grace. It was a faery.

The faery parted its pointed lips and laughed at her. No sound came. Asria reached for it in the darkness, her dress falling long into the pools of the Highlands beneath. They rose up together, the creature's wings lighting over her bare shoulders, the golden dust of pixies falling into her eyes, and her hair. The thick tresses of her hair cascaded below her feet, mingling with the hair of the faery. She felt the rush of air on her face with the beat of the wings, both of them spiraling together in their invisible embrace. The legs of the faery grew, the muscles pulling longer than those of any man. They danced wildly through the sky, the stars glittering eyes of sprites as they circled the fire. He drew Asria in, his long fingers caressing her neck, his palm winding through her hair. She felt his sweet breath and opened her eyes. His face was angular, his pointed ears and his smile tilted, his lips twisting and puckering as they neared her. His eyes were a violet fire, a purple so rich she forgot herself in their dazzle. He stroked her back, each touch rendering her more and more paralyzed in his arms. He was everywhere around her now, the drums of the sprites beating higher and faster beneath their white palms. His hand wound down her navel, and she shivered. The fire blazed with the wild music, and she gave herself to the dance. He swept her up in his arms, hands sliding over her thighs, his mouth a flutter of whispers and tingle over her ears, her eyelids, her throat. She flew higher in his grasp, her body powerless on the wave of flight. They twirled in the rhythm, his legs growing stronger and winding round hers. Her body fell and he caught her, rushing up beneath her gown to the secret regions beneath. His mouth was in her mouth now, his wings beating up and down her legs and back. His hands slid over her belly and breasts. She had no gown now, only him. She gasped for air, unable to pull away from him, her mouth locked under his lips, her arms and legs held in his enfolding, her legs almost numb with pleasure. The he shot inside. She was no mind, no body, no thought. She was ecstasy, and pure light, and she was that tiny white dot that pulsed beneath her skin.

⁓

"Asrian, I have been for seven days now to your door. Am most anxious.—William"

He posted this note with the others he had left and walked back home. His beard was unkempt, and his haggard face caused many a sideways glance as he passed down the street. He turned into an alleyway and relieved himself. The night was cold, and once back in his room, he poured something to warm himself. He stared forward as he drank, not troubling to light a candle. Minutes turned to hours in the stillness, and though he sat next to the window, he saw nothing.

There was a loud rap at his door. He sprang up, tipping the glass he'd forgotten that he'd held, and threw open the lock. Not one man, but four stood outside his door.

"William Harvey?" Asked one in a deep, thick Italian accent. They wore the uniforms of the Italian police.

"Yes," he answered.

"May we step inside?"

William glanced dully into his room toward the hen roost, and found himself pushed inside. The door closed behind the men and he found himself to be the smallest man in the room, and his thinking very slow.

The man who had spoken to him stood over him now. When he spoke again, the Italian accent was dropped and replaced by something else. The man was English, like William, and high-bred.

"You keep the company of an Asrian McGready, correct?"

William looked from one man to another. He wished fervently he hadn't drunk tonight.

"Is something wrong?" he asked them.

The Englishman continued. "I asked you a question, Sir Harvey."

William raised his hand uselessly in the air and laid it back by his side.

"Yes."

"And where is he now?"

The men were all intent on his answer. His voice came out small. "I do not know."

The largest of the four stepped up to him. He also had an English accent, but cockney. "Come now. You can tell us." The man curled his hand into a fist.

William shook his head. "I assure you, I truly do not know."

The first Englishman was walking around the room. "Mind if we have a look around?"

Without his response, they began their search. They lifted up the thin mattress of his bed. One took out a blade and slit it diagonally across the middle. Another overturned all his stacked books and rifled through the desk. He had only, besides these furnishings, the hens and their paraphernalia. To William's astonishment and protests, they lifted the hens one by one, checking beneath them, and not refastening their cages.

"I really must insist you not tamper with those birds!" He cried. "Those are part of a carefully set experiment. Their conditions are most precarious-" The men ignored him and continued their search.

"Oi!" the cockney yelled. All the men turned. He had overturned the grain bin, and as its contents rushed over the floor, he yanked something shiny and long out of the grain.

"What's this?" the Englishman asked.

"I'm sure I don't know," William said desperately. He had never seen it before.

"Pretty thing for a young student to possess, don't you think?"

William was dumbfounded. The grain had hidden a long fancy scarf, glittering with gold and jewels. He couldn't speak.

The Englishman advanced on him.

"Now then, I think we have a lot to talk about. Let's begin again. Where is your friend Asrian?"

William spied the tall form of Asrian coming up the walk to his door. He dropped the broken remnants of the grain measuring devices and rushed to the doorway. He met Asrian in the walk.

"Asrian, come with me!" he whispered ferociously. He ran at such speed that Asrian had to run to keep up with him, out into the street and to a waiting coach. William lifted up blankets in the back. "Get underneath."

"William, what's going on?"

"Do it, Asrian."

She climbed in, face contorted, with visions of the wagon years past that she had hid in as Robert drove. William drew the blankets over her. She pushed to expose her face.

"What is it, William?"

He finished covering her.

"Your books are in there. And some food." He flashed a look behind him and leaned in to her. "You are not safe here. The British undergoverment is turning over Padua to find you." Suddenly, his face softened, turning to something desperately tender, and he clutched her hand fiercely. "Goodbye, my friend. I love you." He released her and turned.

"But the experiment—I must tell you!" She called.

"You must go! There is no time!"

Without a backward glance, William ran to the front of the coach. "Off!"

The coachman gave the signal and the wheels lurched forward, as the horses thundered down the road.

– 8 –

The Circle is Cast

The coach stopped only a half mile down the road. Asrian heard English voices.

"That'll be all, thanks."

"But sir, I have orders."

"Philip?"

As an answer, Asrian heard the coachman cry out. The coach rocked with the pounding of feet, and without a second to gather her wits, Asrian felt the blanket yanked off her form. A cluster of angry faces bent over her.

"Evening, gentlemen," she said.

❧

Asrian had never been in a jail. They treated her remarkably well, so well, in fact, that she sensed her treatment was unique. She was given tea with milk and sugar, and some biscuits and cheese. This did not look in the slightest like the jail of her imagination. It looked like a proper room which happened to be unfurnished. A storage room, perhaps. No windows. Everything was congenial enough. Although the men had been caught up in the power that their positions as captors had allowed them, they did no more than speak in intimidating tones and hold her arms a bit roughly. Asria was rather enjoying this little adventure and looked forward to seeing what would happen next. The jailers found her asleep in the morning.

"Your presence is required by Her Majesty immediately. You will rise, and be bathed, and brought before Herself."

Asria blinked. The lock was jangled into opening, and she sat upright on the floor.

"Come with me," the man said without really looking at her. She allowed herself to be led. They walked down the long stone corridor.

"Pleasant enough sleeping quarters," Asria was saying. "Revived me utterly. And the food was good, too. In fact, with all of these kind provisions, I feel so refreshed that I doubt that I need a bath. In fact, I feel positively shiningly clean. Do I look unkempt to you?"

The man said nothing, and only continued leading her down the hall. Three men had fallen into step behind them and were keeping time.

"I mean really, a man only needs a bath so often, and it was only yesterday—"

A door opened to a staff of women. Asria could see that this was no horse-and-prisoner-scrubbing stall; this was a true bathing room, with heavy towels and hot, scented water.

Without a word, the men handed Asria to the care of the women. They began their efficient stripping, removing her hat, her coat, her shoes, and began unbuttoning her blouse.

"Really, mum, I'm a bit shy. Perhaps you would let a fellow do the filthy jog himself."

The women seemed not to hear. Asria glanced around, and saw only more peasant hands grabbing at her garments. Asria looked straight into the eye of the older woman removing her blouse. She lifted Asria's arms and pulled it off. Asria was bare. The women made no reaction. Asria raised an eyebrow.

After the bath, Asria was dressed into a simple linen gown. They combed her short hair and scrubbed her nails, both of her hands and feet. They even scented her with oils. Wildflowers, Asria recognized with a twinge of her nostrils.

The women gave her to men, different men, evidently of higher charge, with lavish clothing and hair. Asria was led through corridor after corridor, until she was sure that much time had elapsed.

The corridors became more ornate, the sconces all lit, heavy brocade curtains at every stained glass window. The people who passed her appeared better fed and tended to than the people she was accustomed to seeing on the streets in Italy.

Several attendants stood at rigid attention in front of the room which Asria sensed was their final destination. Not one of them looked at her directly, but one on the end decidedly sneaked a glance her way. Asria laughed.

The men released her into the charge of the chamber attendants, the final round of escort. Wordlessly, they led her through a small waiting chamber and into the main sitting room. Queen Elizabeth stood facing her.

Asria was dazzled by the grandiose elderly woman, pale beyond reason, with her high, high forehead and the traces of once known beauty. Her dresses, the layers, they seemed to go on forever. Asria wondered how she could stand under all the weight. Her collar was a marvel, her neck wrapped and tall, the fan of light golden fiber surrounding her face. Jewels glittered with movements of their own as she stood still. Inside, underneath, she was a tiny, frail thing, Asria could see this, and felt a bit of pity toward the woman.

"Her Majesty," announced a man's clear voice.

Asria realized that she was probably being irreverent and wondered what, exactly, was the proper thing to do. She bent and bowed down to the floor.

"Rise," the Queen said.

Her voice compensated for all of the frailness of her appearance. The timbre was strong, commanding, unquestioning, the sort of voice that commanded and sent one running to follow its order. Her voice told everything, her class, her expectations, her experience, her power. Asria was struck with respect for the woman.

"Leave me with the prisoner," she said.

The room was emptied. The woman looked at Asria, examined her, motioned for her to turn, which she did. Then the Queen sat down, her figure cut majestically by the high-carved back of her chair.

"Sit."

Asria sat on the low sofa across the room.

"What is your name?"

"Asria."

She smiled. "Thank you. And where are you from?"

"Scotland, Your Highness, schooled in Padua University."

Her features did not change. "Do you know why you have been brought here before us today?"

"I do not, Ma'am."

Elizabeth reached to the table beside her and lifted something from it. Asria saw that it was the scarf. She felt her eyes widen, realizing that someone had discovered it in the grain bin and stolen it. And it had seemed like such a good hiding place, she thought ruefully.

"Where did you get this?"

"It was given to me at birth, in a trunk, which I have carried all of my life, unopened until very recently."

"And what made you open it at that point?" She fingered the scarf with something more than idleness, staring at its design.

Asria shrugged. "Well, you know, curiosity does get the

best of one, eventually."

The Queen lifted her head sharply.

"You have been truthful with me until now. Do not attempt to deceive me. Remember where you are."

Asria sighed. She felt her shoulders lower.

"Your Highness, I am conducting a most important experiment in cooperation with one of my colleagues. It was imperative to me for medical, as well as personal reasons, that in order for me to continue in the experiment, I know as much of my background as possible." She looked at the Queen, whose face betrayed nothing, only she was listening to her steadily. "I was orphaned and raised by a man in the Scottish highlands. I know nothing of my origins."

She waited, but Asria had nothing more to offer.

"And do you now know nothing of your origins?"

Now Asria looked steadily at the Queen. Her glowing white face, her wise eyes, put Asria at ease somehow. She felt that she understood this woman and could be understood by her. She wanted to make herself very clear and not waste this opportunity. Besides all of this for her own sake, there was the possibility of William's research receiving the true recognition that it deserved. *This is for you too, my friend.*

"I know nothing for certain. Inside the trunk were that scarf, a document from a scholar with appropriate maps, and a chair."

"Chair?" asked the Queen suddenly.

"Yes, Your Majesty."

"What sort of chair?"

"A curule, in fact, an iron study chair now out of fashion. Quite handsome, I think."

Her eyes were busy with thought. "Where is this chair now?"

"Why, it is in my room, at the university."

"I see." She seemed to dismiss the matter utterly at that point, and looked intently at Asria.

"And what else?"

"In the box, why, there was the scarf. And the royal seal of England, on a letter stating "This child must never set foot in England."

"What conclusions did you draw from all of this? "

Asria leaned back into the sofa, lost in her own exasperation. She looked at the ceiling. "I have no idea. Only the document indicated that once there existed an island, an island off the coast of Ireland. It was a land of intellectuals and artists of the highest degree, a peaceful people who kept their own libraries, a sort of collective observer of the rest of the world. They brought nearly no one in, and continued their descendants from their own line. In this way they achieved the breed of thinkers that they all desired and desired to be." She looked at a portrait on the wall and recognized it as King James. "I do not do it justice. It sounds, wonderful, really, lyrical, a sort of haven for peaceful life and study."

"What is the name of this island?" asked the Queen. She was looking at the scarf in her lap.

"Daculi."

The word hung between them and filled up the room, a token of magic, a charm that held promise in its echo. The sound sang its shadow into existence in the tiny, glitteringly cluttered, stone-walled room. The Queen turned her head and looked straight into Asria's eyes with a look of determination that made Asria sit upright.

"You have been honest with me. You are commendable. Your friend Harvey thinks highly of you, as do your professors and fellow students. Feel at ease here."

Somehow, the important tone of introduction she used made Asria suddenly brace herself. What she had just said was stated earnestly enough, but in the throw-away tone of one who has prepared something much more vital to say.

"You neglected to mention that these people were also known as witches, by people who did not understand what they were seeing. And in conclusion, their island was burned.

That was the end of their line, yes?"

Asria shook her head in question.

"No. It was not the end. Your ancestors are Daculi "witches." When the island was raided, only two persons escaped from the entire nation, a man . . . and a woman." She paused for a moment. "The woman fell into my disfavor. She is no more." Her voice betrayed nothing, but Asria detected something peculiar in her eyes which she could not name. In an instant, it was erased, and she continued.

"The man made his way to England, and because of his exceptional scholarliness, and falsified background which he himself contrived, was admitted into this kingdom. His name was William Grindal, and he was a tutor to King James and to Me." She spoke with intense focus, but no emotion. "Grindal and I loved each other. It was forbidden and secret. Grindal was murdered. I gave birth to a girl. That girl was you."

Asria heard the words, but as if they were being said to someone else, in a play, perhaps, or a story in a book. She felt nothing, but felt at the same time sent into suspension, hovering in limbo in between the Queen's words.

"You were shipped away to the Highlands. I wonder that I didn't have you killed. It was some moment of maternal instinct, I suppose."

Asria continued looking at her.

"You are now pregnant with your own child."

Asria did feel a definite reaction to this, shock and a rush to defend. Elizabeth raised her finger.

"Most would have you killed now that you know all of this." She lowered her hand back onto the chairarm. "But I am not going to do this. You are the only bridge to the power of Daculi. You are the last and final link. I know, from Grindal, the beauty of such nature. He was wise, and he was gentle. And beautiful."

She removed herself from her reverie and looked at Asria. "You, too, are beautiful, and with much of him. I can see it in your every movement and hear it in your words. This line must continue. Your child is begotten of witchcraft—"

"Science." said Asria. "Science. Call it what you like, but there are basic, scientific principles here that have produced this result. The power of thought, and will, and all the laws of reproduction which William has so carefully researched and brought out."

Elizabeth was watching her. Asria felt this examination and halted, her words being lost.

Elizabeth nodded. "You did not inherit such impulsive violence from your Father. I see that you also hold Me."

Asria was silent.

"But with his sense of restraint. Good. Now, I will not be interrupted again. This child is begotten of what the world will ignorantly regard as the common idea of witchcraft. If you are found out, you and it will surely be killed. You will be accused of bargaining with the Devil and working magic. This much, the magic, you did do."

Asria's teeth set. Elizabeth looked privately amused.

"You followed the practice of true witchcraft; that is, you used the insight of science, the procedure of intellect, and the power of your own will drawing on nature. You have used your full power, in thought, in knowledge, and in magic.

"My child, you are a Daculi witch.

"And this line must not be lost. You have made it possible to keep it alive. You have a duty now, a responsibility as a teacher and a vessel and a mother. You will be sent to a private island stocked with the best of all books and research, and you will continue Daculi. You will teach your children the trick which you discovered, and in that way, continue the line. Each of them will continue the line. I will provide whatever materials and servants, within reason, that you require."

She smiled and held open her arms.

"Now, child, come to Me, and grant this old woman a moment of communion with Her child."

Asria rose, walked slowly toward Elizabeth, and bent to kiss her hand. Elizabeth clutched Asria's hand and they looked long and deep into one another's eyes.

"The Daculi Witches," said Asria, "will live on."

Afterword

It's not what you look at that matters, it's what you see.

—*Henry David Thoreau*

How much of this book is factual?

Although this work is fictitious, the characters it is based upon are real. Queen Elizabeth was tutored by Sir William Grindal. They were not lovers, nor is there any reason to doubt Elizabeth's renowned identity as a virgin. This story invents, and it makes use of gaps in history, such as how Elizabeth learned the tragic story of her mother, the nature of the flirtatious relationship between her and Tom Seymour. The letter which Elizabeth wrote to her father in apology for some unknown offense is referenced in chapter one.

The island of Daculi did exist—at least in several navigational maps. The Medici map of 1351, the Pizigani map of 1367, Beccario of 1435, and the Pareto of 1455 all show the same exact location of this island off the coast of Ireland. Today it remains one of history's mysteries.

Angelica Laem is purely fictitious, but the Wisharts are not. Janet Wishart was the most prominent accused witch of the sixteenth century Aberdeen Witch Trials. She was indicted for bewitching Alexander Thompson to ail and Andrew Webster to die.

Gilly Geillis Duncan was a servant girl to David Seaton, who thought that her skills for curing "all such as were troubled or grieved with any kind of infirmity," were of the Devil. This began the sweeping panic of the North Berwick Witch Trials, with tortures and deaths more gruesome than any described here.

William Harvey attended Padua after leaving Cambridge, and there began his famous work on the circulatory system, the heart, and blood. Before that, though, he was quite engrossed with the question of reproduction, for the actual "how" of the process had not yet been determined. Chapter Seven quotes passages from his arguments and studies on reproduction; however, there is no indication that Harvey ever toyed with the notion of autoreproduction.

About the Author

Kat Ricker has won awards for journalism, poetry and short stories and is a recognized freelance fitness writer. Kat was named in the Year's Best of Fantasy and Horror, Eighth Annual Collection.

Her other books include *Doubting Thomas*, a suspense thriller examining the dark side of saintliness in the Catholic Church; and *Something Familiar*, a collection of short stories and poetry.

Kat holds a master's degree in professional writing from Slippery Rock University in Pennsylvania and has taught writing at Washington State University and various colleges.

Her website is www.MightyKat.net.

Other Titles by Kat Ricker

from
 Trillium Press

Available on Amazon.com

Doubting Thomas
ISBN 978-0-615-31849-3
$8.95

In a time of change in the Catholic church, a priest in a crisis of faith discovers in a young boy a living relic, a mystic, a saint. But the world is not so sure. Pitted against a family desperate to escape their secret nightmare and the public that cannot understand what he does, this priest must do all in his power to guard the boy against the world and against himself... including the ultimate, horrific sacrifice.

Something Familiar
Poems and short stories
ISBN 1-590281-52-7
$10.00

This collection embraces storytelling about characters you'll recognize, from life in smalltown America, the farm, to the strange conversations of otherworldly matters heard on the metro bus, and even a fairy or two.

Watch the trailers at www.MightyKat.net